Clear Blue Silence

A NOVEL BY

Allan H

KTAV PUBLISHING HOUSE

Clear Blue Silence

KTAV PUBLISHING HOUSE
527 Empire Blvd
Brooklyn, NY 11225
www.ktav.com
orders@ktav.com
Ph: (718) 972-5449 / Fax: (718) 972-6307

Set in Arno Pro by Raphaël Freeman MISTD, Renana Typesetting

ISBN 978-1-60280-476-0

Printed and bound in Israel

To Penny and Bob Morris

Special thanks to Lydia D'moch

"When we ask for advice, we are
usually looking for an accomplice."

— *Saul Bellow*

CHAPTER ONE

The somber sounds in late September on Long Island seemed familiar and flat, if not nostalgic. I grew up here. All of my young bruises and joys happened east of Manhattan. Yet for a split second inside my ear there was an unworldly siren, like a rabid coyote in rural California. Sometimes the dark noises in my head were of my own doing. I was driving a rental from JFK airport; the seat wouldn't let me adjust a better headrest position and one of the side mirrors had a chiseled crack which looked like a comic book lightning bolt. My first mistake of the day was not inspecting the Toyota from every exterior side. My iPhone's Google map app wasn't necessary but still it was in service if I didn't recognize the correct turn. The GPS inflection was more pleasant than Siri – the smart-girl-next-door who dressed sensibly voiced. My goal today was to attend New Montefiore Cemetery in West Babylon. It was a yearly obligation which I embraced faithfully, having adopted California as my final home. I wondered with each visit how I would handle this if I drove here monthly, perhaps weekly, assuming I kept my residence in Manhattan. In my faux denim sport jacket's left pocket I had a folded black skull cap. A *kippah*. A *yarmulke*. A perfect circle and as powerful as Harry Potter's wand. In my right pocket I had a cloth face mask, also black. An imperfect triangle. A muzzle and a lifesaver. Everything I wore was black, except for my cotton necktie which was a faded sky blue and frayed at the tip. My tattered tie was my favorite one. There were cumulus clouds hanging low, moving quickly with the early autumn winds. I felt less lonely because of the soft clouds. Rain would have been welcomed, to cleanse the day.

The visit inadvertently was timed between Rosh Hashanah and Yom Kippur. The week's solemnity was universal among practicing Jews. I was more Jewish during this short interval. The drive along the commercial segment of Wellwood Avenue can be monotonous and even hypnotic. Traffic was light. I counted a half-dozen monument and gravestone merchants, and three florists with outdoor bouquet table displays. One Greek diner with a broken neon sign had an old Volkswagen bus blocking the parking lot entrance. Large industrial vehicles lumbered along Wellwood between Southern State and Northern State Parkways. Tumultuous trucks heard against the stillness of cemeteries. This felt like some pulse of life. Workers and undocumented day laborers hold things together along these adjacent cemeteries straddling Southern State Parkway. Legendary Robert Moses was credited for the aesthetically posh stone bridge parkways, blocking commercial traffic from using these thoroughfares designed for the newly minted middle class. Moses was known as The Master Builder of all things public and out of proportion in New York State. Nearly every towering causeway and bridge were his, but never a bridge too far. Moses was born a Jew and raised a secularist. It would have been far more profound if he were born a secularist and raised a Jew. He converted to Christianity, died in 1981, and was interred within a crypt of an outdoor mausoleum in The Bronx's Woodlawn Cemetery. If I were ever to meet Robert Moses in the hereafter ambassador lounge, I wonder whether or not I would even be able to recognize his granite face. Probably I would ask him if he regretted being responsible for causing the beloved Brooklyn Dodgers to move to Los Angeles. Nonetheless, Shea Stadium landed in Queens just in time for The Beatles' invasion of America. Moses laid to rest in the Bronx – the Engineering Prophet for Profit. Wrong boroughs for both. Not that I was ever a big Dodgers fan, but I have roots in Brooklyn and Moses was credited for destroying tawdry Coney Island, despite the penetrating, sideshow portrait photography of Diane Arbus and the annual Coney Island Mermaid Parade in June.

Four years ago my mother passed away. My father passed away four decades ago. I remember as if it were yesterday driving with both parents along Wellwood to take in the open land cemetery at the time – New Montefiore – established in the late 1920s. My parents told me, their only child and a depressed teenager, that this was their designated final place of rest. It was a durable, practical announcement akin to hearing someone's next car will be a Tesla. My family didn't argue with progress. Someday we just end, and that was progress. This was my father's philosophy. My parents had purchased two grave sites side by side. A romantic notion to some and also a spiritual yearning to distant, knowing eyes. Old Montefiore Cemetery, in Queens twenty-five miles west, was approaching capacity burials at the end of the 1970s. That's not a newspaper fact but a reasonable thought. Land was finite. Memory more finite. To the metropolitan Jewish community, Old Montefiore seemed famous, rather prestigious, and clearly more populous, in part due its proximity to Manhattan and the generations of burials. Several Jewish mobsters were properly buried at Old Montefiore: Abraham Telvi and the brothers Hyman, Joseph and Louis Amberg. The Ambergs excelled at organized crime and filial unity. Something to pitch to Netflix and Adam Sandler if I turned to screenwriting. A whole series devoted to Jews who avoided medical school. Many Jewish mobsters had masqueraded as charming enterpreneurs. The tough fisted Jewish boxer Al "Bummy" Davis' grave can be found at Old Montefiore along with the stupendous actor Fyvush Finkel who crossed over from Yiddish Theatre, renowned International Relations scholar Hans Morgenthau, and painter Barnett Newman who was known to have worked in his father's clothing business before rebelling. In the more rural New Montefiore, indomitable towering New York City mayor Abe Beame (5' 2" and New York's first observant Jewish mayor) and conductor/composer Morton Gould host their grave sites. I learned recently that hard-driven journalist and lifelong Communist Moissaye Joseph Olgin was buried in New Montefiore plus legendary punk rocker Tommy Ramone (né *Tamás Erdélyi*), drummer for The Ramones. I had met one of The Ramones at the Tribeca Film Festival which was a modest thrill. Old and

New Montefiore brought harmony to the cosmos with these curious pairings of deceased souls.

I carried New Montefiore's torn ground map in my pocket in case I confused the three lanes that would lead me to my parents' gravesite. I didn't need to check the map most visits. But there were occasions where I had no bearings. My sense of direction would crumble whenever I got knots in my stomach. I parked the Toyota by the curb that was edged along the tight row near Sinai and Maimonides lanes. I could count only ten dispersed cars on the drive along the route to my family site. One car – a Chrysler van – let out several well-dressed little girls and their mother wearing a serious hat. The image was the equivalent of a Jewish Renoir canvas.

Walking slowly to the gravesite I was startled to see a disrupted contour on the north edge of my mother's grave. There seemed to be either a minor landslide or some effort by groundskeeping to shift the landscaped hedges which crowned her plot. My father's grave was untouched. I looked around to check if other graves experienced any land shifting, but it was only my mother's grave. This was very unsettling. I took out my phone to photograph the damage and made certain that I showed every angle. I imagined telling my mother that this problem would be addressed before the weekend. Certainly before Yom Kippur. The thought occurred to me that this disruption was an act of vandalism. I had heard that some Jewish cemeteries in New York and Connecticut were dealing with vandals. I emailed the photos to myself in case I lost my phone despite my constant forgetting that Apple sends everything to the cloud. The cloud was society's new safety guarantee and humanity's successful attempt to create heaven for a fee of $4.99 per month.

I remained at the gravesite for a brief time. I placed a small stone on each monument. This was a Jewish custom of making a symbolic connection, perhaps expressing a belief that the deceased was now with God. There were several rocks on both headstones. Family members and friends paying respect. I walked back to the car unsure about my dialogue with parents invisible, unsure about my dialogue within myself. The Jewish head covering went back inside my jacket pocket and I drove off. Leaving New Montefiore was easy with the exit markings apparent. It was time to return to my motel and fall over the bed, admitting dull emotional exhaustion. I was aware of my unfinished conversations with my mother and with my father.

Long Island chain motels came in two models, since they never pretend to be hotels: avoidable and unavoidable. I shun the inexpensive motels for hygienic reasons, however when I was very young I loved cheap sheetrock roadsides. The superior models have odorless rooms and WiFi which work successfully by the toilets. At check-in, I made it a practice to ask that the room be far from the ice machine, far from the elevator, far from the pool entrance, far from the cleaning supply room, far from the courtesy business center, far from the breakfast buffet, and of course far from the rear motel entrance where forgettable felonies are condoned. This usually leaves a dozen rooms which I often fail to get. I usually get the ice machine terrain. In dopey self-hypnosis, I repeat the mantra: ice is nice. I refused to book a business hotel.

My daughter left a voicemail on my phone. This was a surprise. A long message. She needed a large sum of money.

My son left a text message too. This was expected. A short message. The toilet was running because the rubber stopper was misaligned.

I am a university professor who has taught film studies for thirty years. Film analysis over generations was literature of a high magnitude, but the tide has turned. I should have remained in the field of aesthetic philosophy where gravity held my feet firmly to the surface of the earth. I had realized eons ago that serious philosophy was a blind career alley and yet film had lost pertinence as civilization succumbed to TikTok. Our movie theatres were closing permanently as quickly as our book stores. Although I truly loved Sarah Cooper lip synching Trump, it seemed that China had the knack to control the next big thing in fifteen second vines. Films once required viewers to commit to a long seating, concentrated viewing. This was a realm of vested culture. All that had changed overnight as our world had *sheltered-in-place* within our air-conditioned living tombs. Riding an elevator with a mask-less stranger became a risk of receiving a death sentence. We were fighting the plague of the century.

My public university had been facing a myriad of challenges ranging from sinking state budgeted finances to the federal government's attack on thousands upon thousands of bright, undocumented students. Perhaps I carried the campus' problem in my heart for all the wrong reasons. This became even more clear during this visit to the East Coast. Acknowledging this need not imply that nihilism had possessed me. However it loomed nearer to nihilism than pessimism, two different and distinct flags.

I journeyed to New York to see cousins and old friends, to see the edifices and grand public spaces of a great city, despite the contagion. It was also on my mind to pay a courtesy call to a former brilliant student Yunmei Yang, who was admitted to Columbia's graduate program a year prior to the Coronavirus. She had sent me a short film that she made to complete a class assignment. The film was haunting and stuck in my mind like a scarred childhood trauma. Her editing was sophisticated as was her attention to visual details. There was no dialogue, only a brief poem at the start of the film. Yunmei composed her soundtrack on a Chinese string instrument. What her work did pierced me but I sensed that the impact, the effect, the intrusion hit like a time-released prescription. Yunmei, in conversation and in her artistic output, had not shown herself to be aggressive, pugnacious, or in the slightest way malevolent. She had struck me as the embodiment of Kant's notion of disinterestedness in his *The Critique of Judgment*, which would be the quality of consciousness prior to cognitive and societal education. Kant imagined that aesthetic judgments had four salient attributes. First, we came from a realm of disinterest, meaning that we should find pleasure in something because we sensed it beautiful, rather than judged it beautiful with our adapted learning. The next attributes were based on the universal and the necessary meant nothing to a bartender or a tax accountant. But because of the intrinsic part of judgment, we would expect others to agree with us. Was beauty in the eye of the beholder? That may not conform to our behavior. We differed over artistic opinions and those who argued skillfully may influence opinion. Beauty, to Kant, was perceived as real property of the *objet d'art* like its size, weight and molecular identity. Universality and necessity would then be elements of our mind. Kant named these qualities to be our "common sense". There need not be objective tangibles of making something beautiful. Finally, in our judgments of art, beautiful things could appear to be "purposive without purpose" – like Marcel Duchamp's urinal and Andy Warhol's Campbell soup cans circa 1962.

Yunmei Yang did not care for Andy Warhol and what she called Warhol's shallow, commercial depth. It was one of the first things she conveyed during office hours. The only Warhol piece that she honored was his acrylic screenprinted *Electric Chair*. Yunmei did not love can soup and was bored by the painted tomato soup cans. I once offered to her the facile equivalence of Warhol's silk screens with Marcel Duchamp's urinal. That had triggered a furious debate down the proverbial rabbit hole. Duchamp's initial plan was to mount the utilitarian urinal on a gallery wall. Yunmei asked me playfully if Americans tried to use the urinal during the first exhibition in New York. Maybe a drunk attendant made the effort. Maybe Duchamp had hoped for that outcome. Duchamp's provocative piece was submitted in 1917 to the Society of Independent Artists. It was the inaugural exhibition by the Society at The Grand Central Palace, but the urinal entitled *Fountain* failed to be placed in the public main viewing area. Following Duchamp's elliptical debut, Alfred Stieglitz photographed *Fountain* and it was immediately published in the Dada journal *The Blind Man*. The original porcelain urinal had not yet been found a century later and that fact may be one of the greatest mysteries in the art world, if not the world of modern, indoor plumbing.

Several weeks later at the end of spring school term and almost eighteen months before the Coronavirus was discovered in Wuhan, Yunmei came to my office hour with a 3 by 5 index card. She wrote most of her dense notes in longhand on cards. She read from the cards that day. "Urinals can be traced to the 9th century. They introduced hygienic measures to communities thousands of miles apart.

However, it was the American industrial revolution that made urinals ubiquitous. Factories hired hundreds of men, which forced factory floors to accommodate toilet space. Relying on urinals, less toilet space was required."

She then directed me to see a painting, found in her cell phone among many impeccable paintings, with the composition of a row of circus clowns pissing along a lengthy restroom wall. The colors were garish and the grotesque entourage was facing the portrait artist while their bodies were squared discreetly towards the urinals. This was not the standard issue showing a dozen clowns surfacing from a tiny car.

"Did you paint this recently, Yunmei?"

"I did." she replied.

"How charming."

"It's not charming, professor."

"Well, certainly this is a witty concoction."

Silence. I struggled with a new question.

"Did clowns pose for you?"

"I suffer nightmares. I am terrified of clowns." This was said just above a whisper.

"So am I." I said.

The conversation veered to the murderer John Wayne Gacy who painted in prison from 1982 to 1994. He was notorious for expressing himself in the visage of a lascivious clown. Gacy, obsessed with his repulsive self-portraits, once worked in clown costumes at children's birthday parties. Months before his Illinois execution, the Tatou Art Gallery in Beverly Hills listed three dozen of his paintings for sale. She knew his whole rap sheet. Yunmei told me that American studios made not one but two horrendous films about Gacy.

"America is a sick nation." I offered.

"China is just as sick. With less freedom."

"Yes."

"But you haven't visited China."

"I will one day."

"When?"

I smiled like a liar.

8

"You won't like China." Her voice rose. "There are cameras at every street corner."

"Did you watch the Gacy movies?"

"No. But I would with you." I laughed in a forced manner. "You're kidding?"

"To see your reaction, professor. You frown like a Muppet."

"I don't like bio pics. I'm against the death penalty, Yunmei."

"Why?"

"Because the State has no moral authority to take a life."

"My mother is a doctor in Shanghai."

"I know."

"She used to oversee executions. She works for the government. Right out of medical school, her job was handed to her. She also supervised other doctors who care for prison women. I think she changed over the years. She won't tell me anything more about her work. There was a time she was involved in examining prisoners before they were killed by lethal injection. China abolished the death penalty for most crimes in 2011. Some years later, my mother got into trouble with the government during clinical tests on a new cancer treatment. She had blamed the government for being reckless with human studies in a rural communities."

"That's serious."

"Yes. She had to retract her criticism."

"Your father is a doctor too?"

"Yes. Medical research."

"What's his focus?"

"Making money. Ha, ha, ha. Vaccines. But he's now like my mother."

"Secretive?" She nodded stoically. "Do they expect you to go to medical school?"

"What do you think?"

"But you won't go?"

"China doesn't need martyred doctors. I'm a martyr to my madness." She glanced around my cramped office. She was eyeing the books on my shelves and checking the family photos along the wall. There were never enough martyrs – was my unspoken thought.

"Do you want to be a filmmaker, Yunmei?"

"Yes. No. I don't know. Painting quickly frees me. But I want to make a million dangerous films. This month I am empty. The films I have made are from desperation. I think I was born in hell. When I was a little girl, my photos showed only chubby angels." My phone rang but I ignored it.

"Would you prefer to be a painter?"

"Yes, that would be enough. I can hide and paint." Her words were heavy like black kettle weights.

"Your images are strong." I said. "And lodged in your personal privacy."

"That's all we have. Privacy."

"We each have more than privacy, Yunmei."

"We have noise. We have silence. Loneliness. Why do you teach?"

"I like to teach. It's a job which has purpose. Smart students make it all worth teaching."

"Can I have office hour next week?" She said this in the most peculiar tone, and her English was suddenly stilted. "Of course."

"Thank you. Same time good."

"Yes, same time is good."

"You like me."

"I like you, yes."

"And Trump?" she asked.

"Trump? What about him?"

"How did he become President? An orange clown. A white racist. I hate him. I hate his family. Why does your country wish to lose all that you won? Why ridicule science and democracy? Why die by your own hands?" I became speechless. Sometimes Yunmei channeled other characters in conversation. There was a gap of time while she kept talking. Yunmei assumed I was attentive as I lapsed into inattentiveness. She described the next short film she wanted to make. The theme would be college suicide and the location in Manhattan – her high inflection emphasized. I had asked why this topic and why hurt people with a message about self-death.

"I fight depression." she said. "Just like you do."

"I'm not depressed."

"You just don't want to admit it, professor. We live after death. Even if our bodies are meant for cold worms in the soil. But we go into the air like pollen in the spring. I know this in my heart."

"That's sadly beautiful, Yunmei."

"It's not about beauty...we just go into the air. Like sea salt. Over the ocean. Into dark space between dead stars. Some call that fucking hell. I hope you never go there."

I was taken back when she said 'fucking hell'. She had referenced this 'fucking hell' obliquely before, the first month I met her. Yunmei had linked her mother once to this blistery, Godforsaken zone. There was some political punishment her mother had to endure some years back. She took out her cell phone and showed me a black and white photograph of a prepossessing young woman. Her final words of the day were that she hated knowing her face was the twin image of her mother's.

CHAPTER TWO

When my wife died in the hospital at 3am, I was on sabbatical working from home. This was a few months after my mother's passing. Traci had stage four pancreatic cancer. It was discovered quite late and in my view she was too young to be so stricken. The hospital couldn't delay the ravishes of this insidious disease. Her passing was a few days before the 2016 presidential election and the pain of her death far outweighed the bitter news that Hillary Rodham Clinton lost to Donald J. Trump. If I became numb from the trauma – to country and to my family – this helped me to cope inside my emptiness. Yes, there was a history of cancer in Traci's family. She was weeks away from turning fifty-seven and never missed an annual physical. Traci was a head librarian at the university and dearly enjoyed her profession. She was a superb advocate for necessary acquisitions. Her colleagues named the staff lounge in her honor three years ago, having lobbied the campus bureaucracy.

Traci's presence was with me in New York but more manifest during the visit to New Montefiore, as if her spirit were Virgil to my Dante. Imagining her lively, playful voice inside my head turned me into a functional creature. She once joked during our honeymoon that I would survive her despite my being seven years older. She once joked that I would not see her in purgatory for my destiny was an ascent above high punishing gates. Cancer was a demon. Traci was strict about her instructions to be cremated, although I had truly yearned for her to have a gravesite.

Parenting two teens without Traci proved overwhelming, but it felt easier whenever I travelled. Our family of three required distancing tricks and helpful neighbors. Still, I loved the role of a father. When the kids were young, from toddlers to kindergarteners, days and nights enveloped the magical. Bedtime wasn't hard. Bedtime meant story time. Lights out, tippy toe. Job well done. Peace.

For this visit to the East Coast there was some pending business despite the pandemic. It wasn't my academic publishers or a pressing personal matter, but someone from my father's world of auto sales had contacted me suddenly with persistence. The phone calls had reached a threshold and I had to resolve a debt. My father drew financing from various quarters and his respectable business was once rumored by my cousins to be spiced by a leaf or two of illegality. Among his bene-factors, there were airs of Sinatra and the 1960s rat pack – heavyset Jewish family men who had hidden profiles when away on company junkets. The alleged vices were predictably high paid escorts, private club gambling, and betting on jai alai in Miami.

One would have thought that these aged legends with surnames like Adler, Berkowitz, Finkel, and Goldstein have now succumbed to Alzheimer's, pacemakers, prostate failure, and curvatures of the spine. Nonetheless, one man was still acting in his prime and it appeared that I was now obligated to see Benny Edelmann. Big Benny. The Bronx Baron. Mr. Bruiser. A handful of Jewish baby boomers in New Jersey, Connecticut and New York knew about the notorious Benny Edelmann. He evaded law enforcement like Adam Clayton Powell Jr. and, like the former Congressman who represented Harlem, Benny had attended the City College of New York briefly.

I remember so well his large brick house in Great Neck – a guy with no neck – his penchant for pet swans, lawn jockeys, cantilever decks, and excessive garden fountains. His desire was to turn every piece of his real estate into royal estate. Boychik Benny. Gangster Benny. Entrepreneur Benny. Cantor Edelmann. He was revered at one reform, Long Island synagogue for having a perfect baritone – the Jewish Vic Damone. The fat alpha male with stubby fingers, chin like a boulder, in wool vests and collarless shirts, and a slight limp, who used to beat everyone mercilessly at poker or at the pool table in the better North Shore bars. Benny made money the old fashioned way by never paying taxes. He boasted he had no social security card and scoffed at Medicare. He had perfected the traceless bribe and claimed that many Long Island police detectives were on his payroll. He was married seven times in strict Jewish ceremonies, twice to the same batty woman Letti who was a distant cousin to hotelier Leona Helmsley – the Queen of Mean who died in 2007. Letti, like Leona, left wrapped and unwrapped chocolates on people's pillows whenever she and Benny were visiting.

My father was able to establish his successful auto dealership in the 1970s mostly through a startup loan from Benny. Maybe it was fifty thousand bucks. Maybe it was a hundred grand. Maybe much more than that. My father never told me exactly. Besides the phone calls, Benny wrote me a letter – in longhand – hinting that there was something unfinished between my father and him. He conveyed that he waited for my mother to pass away before contacting me and then the matter slipped from his memory. Benny Edelmann's need to write was expressed by his bizarre sentence structure and how he underlined phrases that had emotional resonance. I assumed that this was more complicated than a minor debt older than Bon Jovi and other 1980s New Jersey bands. Benny gave out loans free of interest to his favorites, and low interest loans to the rest of mankind. Usury is one of the cruelest things society endures and dozens of dissertations delve into the vortex between Shylock and the practice. Benny Edelmann's letter was crumbled in my suitcase. I couldn't toss the letter away. I was superstitious.

Atria Park of Great Neck was Benny's current address. The seniors' facility was assisted living only. I had guessed that Benny's age was between eighty and eighty-eight. He survived his wife Letti ten years ago but went the route of assisted living after a serious car accident on Throggs Neck Bridge upon leaving Mamaroneck. One of my father's friends had sent me the Newsday clipping with a Christmas card that made gentle fun of Hanukkah. The card also referenced Benny's only son Max. I vaguely remember Max Edelmann, close in age to me, with anger issues and the posture of a cartoon lampost. Max had his extravagant bar mitzvah featuring an all-Broadway-musician orchestra in Little Neck, creating a punning pattern on a scruff neck motif.

Because of COVID health precautions, no one was allowed to visit Atria unless they were immediate relatives and older than twenty-one. Benny must have paid off the security staff, because I was allowed to check in at the front desk. On the visitor sheet which I had to sign with the pen chained to the desk, I was identified as Mr. Edelmann's *other* son. Nonetheless, Max Edelmann was Benny's scion. I wore a N95 face mask newly removed from a wrapping.

"You've been here before…" said the staffer, thinner than a Gap store mannequin and equally expressive. "Actually, no. First time."

"Your father is expecting you."

"How is he?"

"Okay. Grumpy. Considering." It was evident this man at the desk was paid off by Benny and I only had to find my way to Benny's apartment door. "Apartment number – 302?"

"That's right. Down the hall, past the lobby and lounge, find the elevator. Atria asks that you keep visits short."

"Under thirty minutes?"

"Under thirty minutes, yes." he said calmly and passed the hand sanitizer to my side of the counter. I cleansed my hands with care and hesitated. I wanted to ask if indeed Benny had a stroke after the car accident, but that seemed too much to press. The staffer held up a handgun thermometer to my forehead. Having no fever, he waved me on. I found the elevator. Not a soul was to be seen in the lounge. There was a faint scent of Noxzema or a mild chemical in the air. I noticed a copy of Monet's waterlilies on the wall opposite the elevator. The frame was tilted ever so slightly and I corrected the angle.

I rang Benny's doorbell and checked the fit of the N95 over my mouth and nose. I heard footsteps. He opened the door and smiled like a vaudevillian backstage.

"Come in *boychik*." Benny's voice was rough and a low bass. Gone was the famous baritone grace. His eyes seemed rather yellow, signaling a condition of jaundice or glaucoma? "Hello Benny. You remember me." "Yeah. Come in. Take off your shoes. I don't care if your feet stink." I entered. Kicked off my loafers. His heavy hands reached for my shoulders affectionately. He closed and locked the door with some effort. Benny was still missing a neck and Adam's apple, his hooded eyelids exaggerated by life's merciless gravity.

"Why did your mother name you Jonathan?" he asked. "I don't know. Haven't a clue." Benny laughed and he coughed. He had no face mask. "Your father never liked naming you Jonathan. Did you know that? Sit down. He wanted to call you Mickey. Treat you like you're Irish. You drink scotch?" I sat down. He brought two glasses of scotch neat. Ice would have been nice.

"Your father was the only guy in the entire world who could make me laugh."

"Thank you." I replied. "I miss him. You know that I really loved your old man." I nodded. I nodded again. I drank from my glass after Benny was finishing a long swallow. "Your father must have told you that I was in legit businesses for many years."

"He did tell me that, Benny."

"And did he tell you that I gave a great deal of money to UJA?"

"Yes." This was United Jewish Appeal. "I gave a lot to Israel's Magen David Adom too." I found myself nodding once more. "I raised money other ways for all these Jewish funds. I *motivate* others, Jonathan." He walked slowly to the thermostat on the living room wall. I noticed that one leg was shorter than his other. He adjusted the level and coughed a bit more while I was across the room on the sofa. I was conscious of the coughing and the risks of being inside.

"I like the apartment cool. And this goddamn management overrides my settings. I paid the custodian Fernando $100 a week to get off their control panel."

"Front desk asks I keep the visit under an hour, Benny."

"Did he say that?"

I noticed a fish tank right next to his mounted television. Tropical fish and an interior light made the aquarium comforting in my anxiety.

"I gave your father a big loan to kick off his business, and he built a terrific company as you know. Interest free. Imagine that. It was a great Chevrolet car dealership before the Japs won the auto war in 1978. I was a good friend of Lee Iacocca, did you know that? When he was with Ford, I pushed him to build the Mustang. He saved Chrysler. Passed away last year. Your father was a great salesman, Jonathan. He read people like a naked book. He was fucking funny. He was persuasive. He did hysterical routines like Jonathan Winters and Robin Williams. Like fucking Sid Caeser. He had a stethoscope inside his jacket for these killer doctor comedy bits with his floor salesmen. Throw your Dad a scarf or an umbrella – you'd get a million improvs. The guy had a ton of charm, *boychik*. Your old man could convert the Pope and in the bargain make him laugh. He was Zero Mostel, Groucho Marx and Gene Wilder rolled into one Jewish gladiator. I gave him money not because he was Mr. Comedy. I gave him money because he was a *mensch* and made me believe there had to be a higher power in the universe if someone could be wired like him. You don't believe me?"

"I believe you, Benny."

"No, you don't. I see your face."

He coughed into his hand. He swallowed some phlegm. His smile was sour. He reached for a box of tissues.

"I believe you."

"When my wife passed away I began to believe in God. That was a big thing. I felt God watching me. I got scared, Jonathan. Someone told me Voltaire began to believe in a Catholic God when he was on his death bed. You know Voltaire, Mr. College Professor. That's like buying flood insurance the night of a hurricane alert. If I were God, Jonathan, I'd give Voltaire a lot of shit at the pearly gates."

Benny laughed like he was getting high on scotch.

"There was a time I wrote down all the loans that were exceptional. The loans that carried no interest. I kept records in a black marble school notebook, like I was back in Eastern District High. Williamsburg. Driggs Avenue. Brooklyn. Where Alan King went to school. The comedian."

"I know, Benny."

"Did you father tell you?"

"About Alan King?"

"About the loan."

"Yes. Decades ago."

"Did he tell you the amount?"

"No."

"Interest free. Nobody does that. Alan King was a mediocre comic, Jonathan. His timing was off and he got away with his Brooklyn attitude. Your old man was a thousand times funnier than Alan King. Your father just needed a talent agent and he would have been the king of Vegas lounges. But fate doesn't make sense. So he was the best salesman of Long Island. Nowadays you buy a silver Tesla and an extension cord from a fucking website. There's no showroom."

"You want me to pay you for my father's debt in installments, Benny?"

There was silence. I heard the air conditioner click on and off.

"No, no, no. I don't want your money. That's not who I am."

Benny finished his drink, got up, and pointed to my drink. I finished my scotch. He made a motion with his fat hand, with his pudgy index finger, the universal sign to follow him. As he opened his apartment door, he donned his cloth face mask with a print design of the American flag and carried a wood broom that was near the front door. I put on my mask and traipsed behind, still shoeless. So was he, shoeless. We proceeded down Atria's endless corridors to one of the recreational rooms that looked like the facility's library and billiards room. Benny flicked on the lighting over the pool table and then he turned to the Amazon Alexa on the oak cabinet. He told Alexa that he wanted classic Sinatra. We got in return, "They Can't Take That Away From Me." This pleased Benny immensely. Benny sang along with Frank. Benny could still carry a tune.

"Take this."

He gave me a cue stick. Then Benny unscrewed the broom head. I knew it was time to get the hell out of Atria.

"You know how I made my first million, *boychik*?"

"Billiards."

He managed to smile showing all of his stained teeth while racking up a standard 8 ball game. Benny unscrewed the broom brush from the wood rod.

"I'll break." he said while holding the broom rod as his cue stick.

Maybe Benny was drunk. I wished I was. His eyes weren't very focused from across the table and he was fidgeting with his patriotic face mask which was clinging to his chin but fell under his bulbous nose.

"Seven ball – side pocket."

He broke the rack and pocketed the seven ball. He put away every ball in quick succession. Benny's bank shots were demonically good. Top spin dominated the table.

"I know," murmured Benny, "you got to get the hell out of here."

"Yeah. How old are you, Benny?"

"I'll be eighty-one in April. Maybe I'm older."

"God bless you, Benny."

He put the broom back together just as Alexa selected "Fly Me To The Moon." We walked back to his apartment. The same staffer was at the front desk and Benny waved to him like a fan in the grandstands. He poured me a second scotch and forced me to sit again on the sofa. He disappeared into his bedroom for about a minute. He reappeared with an overweight calico cat who was making unnatural sounds.

"Your father owed me more than a quarter million."

"Okay."

"You look surprised."

"I am surprised."

Benny's face lifted into a ray of hope.

"This is Cassandra. She's the smartest animal in the galaxy. I'm not allowed to keep pets in this place. Imagine that? I got caught a week ago. By my neighbor. I tried to pay off the fucking neighbor. Good luck with that. My son has allergies. I'm not going to move 'cause I hate moving from place to place."

Benny took out a cat carrier from below the fish tank. He had a bag of dry cat food on the coffee table. He leaned into her head slowly like it was a religious ritual.

"Cassie, Cassie, Cassie…"

CHAPTER THREE

As I signed out of Atria Park Great Neck, the cat carrier was at my ankles. The front desk clerk heard the cat's cries, pretending nothing outrageous was unfolding. It seemed for him and for me that it was smarter to pretend that Cassandra was an imaginary animal. The world needed more imaginary animals. I said a sincere thank you. The electronic glass doors opened and I walked quickly to my car. I felt like the sad bag man in a ridiculous crime film. More tellingly, I felt like one of the shaggy idiots in *Dumber and Dumber*. Because I ran into one of the maintenance men carrying a flash light and also a long ladder outside, and reflexively twirled to avoid getting slammed, I was also the American incarnation of French cinema's superbly balletic Jacques Tati. All that I required was Tati's signature pipe, hat, overcoat and a trenchant eyebrow. I opened the side door of the Toyota rental, placed the cat carrier on the passenger seat, and tried to comfort the loud feline. She was furious about transport and leaving Benny Edelmann.

I was never a cat person. Cat people are a unique species. Cat people don't always use comprehensive words but rely on complex astral chords and knowing looks. They made more than one horror film about cat people perfectly entitled *Cat People* – the 1982 remake was known for the David Bowie tune *Cat People (Putting Out the Fire)*. Traci loved that song. I had suffered the experiences of a male cat in grad school with a roommate who loved Siamese cats. Perhaps there was a powerful symbiosis between my former roommate and his pet.

I recalled that in that dank grad school apartment, there were many nights alone when I thought the cat was reading my mind. Hours of intense study and essay writing led to sessions of trading looks with the Siamese beast named Dvořák who sat on my desk. I practiced tolerance and I believed that the effort had paid off more handsomely than not. When imagining an animal could read my mind, I was feeding my penchant for paranoia and also harmonic convergence. This cat was not a composer. I remember thinking that Dvořák knew I was an inconsistent young scholar and was sensing my potential for mediocrity or modest accomplishment. My cold comfort was knowing that this creature would never tell a living soul, and in return I always filled his faux porcelain dishes when circumstances warranted.

At the brightly lit motel parking lot, I entered through the rear door with my key card. It was better not to declare the cat, assuming pets were forbidden. This was my second and final night at the motor lodge. I had stopped along the way at a supermarket to pick up kitty litter, a plastic laundry basket, catnip, two little ceramic bowls, and a small bag of dry Purina cat food. Purina was on sale. Of course I forgot to take the cat food bag left in Atria's parking lot. Benny said that the tan striped legged beast ate both kibble and can food, but I didn't want to buy wet odorous stuff. Benny swore that quality catnip would render Cassandra ecstatic, intoxicated, and lessen the chance of getting bit by her.

"She likes to nip." The last words out of Benny's mouth.

"So do I."

Once inside the motel room, I put everything down and went to the bathroom. My phone rang but I needed to piss. Cassandra was howling like the girl in *The Exorcist*.

Of course, her mythological name warned others of impending disaster which go unheeded. Once I let her out of the carrier, the motel room took on a new atmosphere that was not quite Joe Exotic's *Tiger King*, yet there was an element of circus. I placed the bowls by the open closet doors. Filled the laundry basket with litter. Unwrapped the catnip. Called the pet's name several times. She jumped on the bed. This cat was aware of the catnip. Maybe it was this moment that we were no longer enemies. I dropped the dope inches from her tail. She made Siamese sounds and contorted her body.

"Chill, Cassandra. I scored for you."

She rubbed her face on the green flakes along the bedspread. All was right in the universe. I didn't have to write a check for $250,000 to Benny Edelmann. He only wanted me to send text photos of the beast every other day until Benny's dementia or Alzheimer's would set in thoroughly. Silent sounds filled my head. My recent suicidal ideations when visiting New York dissipated. On my iPad's Amazon Music app, *Life and Death* by Avishai Cohen played serenely. The jazz piano riffs were resplendent. The haunting piece was a fantastic composition. I forgot all about the pandemic and my lingering tensions at the university. I looked at my phone to see who had called. It was Celeste. She knew I was in New York. I listened to her long message while watching Benny's cat roll along the bedspread. I opened an airplane miniature of Dewer's whiskey, pouring it into a bathroom glass and found myself talking to the cat who looked high. I asked Cassandra if I should call Celeste. But atop the bed she was like Cleopatra's cat. I finished my drink while checking for email and texts from my kids. I flipped a coin onto the bed, skipping off the cat's head. I decided to call Celeste back.

"Hi." I said.

"Jonathan!"

She asked if I were still on the East Coast.

"I was at the cemetery."

"That's what Jews do." we almost said in harmony.

"I tested for COVID." She replied.

"Oh. How did you do?"

"I'm negative. It just takes a day to get results in New York."

"I tested a couple of weeks ago in California."

"You didn't get it?" she asked.

"Well, I did get the virus and didn't know I had it. So I took the serology test. You know, tracking for antibodies. I'm immune now, I think. My kids too. At least for a few months."

"Lucky you."

"That's why I was okay about flying here."

"I think it's the apocalypse, Jonathan."

She laughed. I laughed.

"We'll get over this crap in another year." I said distinctly.

"No, we won't. Even with the damn vaccine, too many idiots won't get vaccinated."

"Maybe the government will pay everyone $500 to take the shot."

"It's not enough, Jonathan. These are big idiots."

She asked me to drive into Manhattan. I said I was tired. She berated me for acting like an old man with gout from Brighton Beach. I replied that all the old folks at Brighton were either Russian mobsters or retired tailors.

"There are open bistros in my neighborhood. I'll buy you dinner."

"You never bought me a meal since we've known each other."

"Really? I've a professional salary, Jonathan."

"I know."

"I'm a valued interior designer."

"You're still married, Celeste."

"That's mostly true."

"Where is Tony?"

"Right here. Quarantine."

"Tony doesn't like me."

"Tony doesn't like anyone. What's your point?"

"Do you need a calico cat, Celeste?"

"There's no traffic on the L.I.E. so just get in your car. I'm right by the Whitney Museum. *Pastis.* 52 Gansevoort Street. I'll see you in an hour."

She hung up.

CHAPTER FOUR

Celeste, looking gorgeous under a dark blue scarf, was waiting at the table. *Pastis* was pleasant, uncrowded, friendly. The lighting was subdued and on the cusp of sepia. She chose well. Celeste appeared older, relaxed, and less flamboyant. Celeste loved her blonde hair long and this was the shortest length in memory. Celeste seemed happy, clear, and centered. She untied her scarf. Her cloth mask hung above a pearl necklace.

"Jonathan."

"Celeste."

I kissed her while she remain seated. She rose and caught me in an extended hug.

"I heard you're moving back to New York."

"Who said that?"

She had on her favorite scent *Trésor*, on the heavy side, and no memory surfaced.

"Someone. Maybe it was Etienne."

"Etienne is a toxic rumor mill. You look terrific."

We sat. She had her glass of white wine at the edge of the table.

"What a fucked-up world, Jonathan. Everyone's afraid to come out of their caves."

"New York's handling it much better. Now the sunbelt has to face the music."

"Cuomo's become a rock star governor."

"We'll see how long that lasts." I muttered.

"You don't age."

"My hair's grey."

"You've kept your hair at least."

The waiter approached with his sleek face mask and Celeste ordered a drink for me.

"I have this recurring dream," she offered in a silky tone, "that the world can't overcome this plague, all the computers crash, looting becomes the norm, and we stockpile rifles."

"That's sweet."

"And money is useless. No one accepts it. Except bitcoin."

I didn't want the conversation to start this way. Our better history was such that intimate family matters would come first in the spirit of emotional inventory. I knew that she had a recent death in her extended family, an older cousin due to the Coronavirus. I told her that I had quickly visited my cousin in Huntington the day before the cemetery. I asked Celeste how her daughter was doing.

"Tanya's fine. She built a healthy private practice and meets with her patients via Zoom. Lives in Park Slope with her boyfriend and dog. I like the dog more than the boyfriend. She was born to be a therapist or an anarchist."

"That's good. She made a practical choice. You get to see her?"

"Yes. For lunch or Sunday walks in the park. She has a drone from the Sharper Image website which picks up dog droppings."

"How's she handling the pandemic?"

"Not well. She hates staying inside. Tanya would love to poison Trump and his minions with a KGB hatpin at his next rally. How are your kids, Jonathan?"

"Barry's finishing high school. Ariel's enjoying her gap year."

"What the fuck really is a gap year?"

"Like paid sabbatical without research. And you get as much sex as you can fit into your year."

"So she's not working?"

"She's a driver for GrubHub and InstaCart."

"Oh."

"Yes, it's come to that."

"You disapprove?"

"I do. She's having unnecessary exposure to people all day even if she stays at a safe distance from the front door."

"Did she have a job before COVID?"

"Restaurant waiter. It paid okay."

"Tips are tips, Jonathan."

Celeste's manicured hands looked whiter than ivory. They occasionally touched my hands. We had a two-year relationship before my children were born and we both made colossal mistakes in hurting each other. We were in love with each other then. Celeste had faulted me for taking the teaching job on the West Coast, even though the move came at an opportune turn. We kept in touch over the years. Facebook made it easier. She knew all the details about Traci's illness. I knew many of the scandalous specifics of her secure, second marriage to Tony DeRosa who graduated from a record-breaking junk bonds broker to a respectable hedge fund manager at Goldman Sachs. It went without saying that squat Tony DeRosa looked remarkably like George Conway's chunky identical twin while Celeste was nothing like the Trump critic's spouse – White House counsel Kellyanne Conway. More to the point, Tony DeRosa was the amoral antithesis of George Conway. In the late 1980s, Tony DeRosa was a protégé of ex-felon Michael Milken but avoided getting swept into the indictments. Chatting with Tony DeRosa generated the feeling of being trapped in a carwash with CNBC's carnivalesque Jim Cramer. I was baffled why she went with him to the altar. She claimed that he was once a tender soul. Unlike DeRosa, Celeste's first husband had dignity and intelligence but that romance had played out as a doomed, semi-arranged marriage by caring friends.

"Why are you in New York?" she asked.

"My frequent flyer miles were about to expire and I lucked out on roundtrip business class upgrade."

"Why are you in New York?"

"I always come out to see my parents before the High Holy Days."

"During the pandemic?"

She didn't accept my responses. Celeste found it easy to think I was withholding. Talking about my father's immense debt to Benny

Edelmann would have taken us down a rabbit hole. So I brought up Yunmei and that pricked her detective muscles.

"Yunmei's an exceptional, young artist."

"How old is she?"

"Twenty-two. She's in a Masters program at Columbia."

"Good for her, Jonathan."

I changed the subject and alluded to Benny as another New York obligation in a senior center. I talked superficially about Benny's colorful criminal life without linking it to filial shame. I managed to make Celeste laugh and thought that would be a great way to end the visit at *Pastis*. I left out the status of the cat in my motel. She brought up the inanities of Jeffrey Epstein's jail suicide and developments with Epstein's associate Ghislaine Maxwell. Celeste claimed that Prince Andrew, Bill Clinton, Alan Dershowitz and Trump would all land in prison eventually. However, Celeste walked back to Yunmei.

"Have you molded this girl into your perfect grad student?"

"No, I haven't."

"Sounds like an erotic escapade." she said with vinegar.

"You know me better than that."

"I do know you well but people change. I thought you carried a torch for me. Honestly. I've saved all your emails. And I'm not drunk, darling. I'm really sorry about Traci's death. You could have called me a week ago before flying here. I know you've got a little storm brewing inside."

"You're not wrong."

I reached out for her hand and there was warmth.

"Did I ever tell you the story," she said, "about my first marriage and our dream house with a view of Long Island Sound? The realtor suppressed information about a murder inside the home. We found out nine months later after living there. I even saw a silhouette of a fiendish ghost."

"Isn't that illegal?"

"Yes. We sued the brokerage and won."

She took back her hand but then kicked me in the shin.

"Are you going to invite me to your motel?"

She smiled at this ability to send a classic mixed signal. I didn't know how to answer her question.

"You didn't sleep with Yunmei yet I'm age appropriate. *Hello, Jonathan.* Cat's got your tongue?"

"Don't play me, Celeste."

"You want to spend the night together."

"The thought is in my head. Yes." I said.

"Well, that's not a bad thought. I would like that. But maybe you're too emotionally intimate with students on route to doctorates?"

"No."

"No?"

"I didn't drive to Manhattan to be your analysand."

"You didn't have to call me."

"I think about you often. You helped when Traci died. I owe you."

She took that internally. The ground shifted.

"Adultery never ends well." I remarked.

"No one likes to define adultery. No one likes getting older. No one likes fucking Thanksgiving or Christmas spent with the wrong people. But we make do, Jonathan. I'm available. You're available. Let's focus on positive things between us. Covid doesn't prevent sex. Why are you in so much pain?"

"Ariel's stealing. She's becoming a thief. I can never give her enough cash. I don't know what to do."

This threw Celeste.

"What?"

"She's into something very weird."

"Shoplifting?"

"I don't know about shoplifting. Teens do that. But she's stealing money. From her brother. From me. From other relatives and neighbors. Hundreds of dollars."

"That's awful, Jonathan."

"It's recent behavior."

"Drugs?"

"Probably."

"A fucked-up boyfriend?"

"Yeah. That's a factor. I could kill him with a projectile toaster oven set to broil."

Our waiter pivoted to us and Celeste ordered another round of drinks.

"Did you confront her?"

"Yeah."

"How did that go down?"

"Like the Hindenburg."

"I'm so sorry."

"I had meetings with her therapist. The prognosis is damning."

"Some therapists are fucking morons."

"Hers is sharp."

"Hard to believe. The last time I saw Ariel she was in middle school and dressed for Halloween."

"I called the police. I've a friend who's a lieutenant."

"And?"

"No good options exist, Celeste."

"You're going to arrest your daughter?"

"No. But option two is just as bad."

"Let me call her, Jonathan."

"That won't help."

"Ariel knows me."

"She'll ask how you got her phone number."

"I don't care. She doesn't have any aunts."

"She'll hustle you for cash."

"No she won't."

"Let me think about it."

"I might make a difference."

CHAPTER FIVE

*P*astis was closing. We were the last to leave. My legs were exhausted and my head was throbbing under a growing migraine. It began to rain ever so lightly. I was gratified to see Celeste and sensed that our history was poignant under the circumstances of a global pestilence. Celeste leaned in for a kiss and we connected with invisible choreography. The street lights were muted. Her breath was sweet. Her lips gave me pleasure and it wasn't perfunctory. Perhaps this kiss was long overdue. She opened her eyes at the end of this public embrace and we probably appeared to each other as bundles of vulnerability. Celeste asked that I call or text her at the airport. She thought she could fly to California once she receives her antibody test. She didn't want a year or more to pass before we could meet again. She referenced Yom Kippur approaching and that all congregations moved online, just as all classroom teaching went virtual for this fall term. It hit me that I specified too many family difficulties. Still, I sensed her care and concern at this time of year. Celeste was half religious, having an agnostic Jewish father who once was observant and an Irish mother who had a complicated dialogue with Jesus.

I found the Manhattan garage, reclaimed my Toyota, applied hand sanitizer on everything, drove from the Midtown tunnel to Queens while the car stereo found the New Jersey jazz station WBGO. I had loved WBGO for many decades. Their playlists were always excellent and every announcer a class act. *Sketches of Spain* from Miles Davis filled my head from the car speakers. I felt twenty years younger. The rain fell harder as I drove.

The motel's parking area was empty. I didn't leave my car immediately. Several thoughts raced by. First among them was that I should hand back the fucking cat to Benny and write out a check from my Merrill Lynch IRA for $100,000. Maybe that would be a down payment. This was about principle and little more. The insurance death benefit from Traci's employer could cover that amount. There was an incongruent symmetry fixing my father's posthumous debt with my late wife's payout. By writing that check and ending all chords to Benny I would regain some power over my life.

A more painful thought darkened things. I seemed to be battling a negative emotion bursting inside, pushing me to flee my own life, maybe abandon the country led by a reality television moron – not revisiting campus teaching, leaving my family and my academic research, abandoning responsibilities grand and small. I was carrying my passport on this trip for TSA airport security, having misplaced my driver's license. Delusional escape fantasies were overwhelming. These urges first emerged at Traci's funeral, reemerged when I met my daughter's latest tattooed boyfriend, and triggered by the freaking cat inside the motel room. My first sabbatical when I had no grey hair was at the Rockefeller Foundation at Bellagio and Italy would be a magnificent destination this month despite the Coronavirus barriers.

I unlocked the motel room door. Cassandra hissed. I whistled back. I imagined Celeste unclothed on the bed and an evening of pleasure. I imagined my father's low octave voice giving me shit about Benny. I imagined the opening stunning minutes of Yunmei's next piece about China's expanding evil where she is talking directly to the camera about Xinjiang Uyghur concentration camps. Her bracing, black and white film pixilated documented faces of Uyghurs – all Muslims living inside China – relying on the sounds of the Chinese historical zither LonQin. Her new work recognized at the Berlin Film Festival. I imagined Yunmei's brutal arrest in late 2021, the first day she went to meet her parents in Shanghai's airport. These fantasies were cascading down. I imagined Ariel's conviction for grand larceny a year from now after a string of beach home robberies throughout San Diego. I ran the shower hot and rinsed off the ugliness in my mind.

The next morning I got out of bed before dawn with back pain, stomach cramps, and a hangover. The air conditioner was on arctic high. The cat was sleeping atop my legs. Purring louder than the A/C. A still life of somnolence and peace. I heard the couple in the next room having loud sex while cursing Christ and the Holy Mother. I could see that I forgot to charge my phone. I knew the day was off to a good start.

The American Jewish community had confronted the High Holy Days on Zoom as if this were the eleventh plague out of Egypt. Zoom turned us into miniscule postage stamps with unstable WiFi issues and Jeffrey Toobin humiliations. The internet was swamped with magical COVID cures, herbs, and prophylactics. Jewish teachings had forbidden the magical, not in so far as magicians be very theatrical or accidentally functional, but primarily due to magic's distraction from the authority of a Supreme Being. God had to be of a higher ordinate far above David Blaine, David Copperfield, Penn and Teller. From Exodus, "You shall not tolerate a sorceress". Technically you can marry a sorceress, but you cannot employ a sorceress. You might be able to divorce a sorceress, but God help you if you try to fire one. The price would be too injurious.

I remember a synagogue sermon from my boyhood on the first three plagues to ruin ancient Egypt. Clearly there was the headline match between Pharaoh and Moses. My rabbi highlighted the background battle between the court magicians and Moses' brother Aaron. The contest was not dissimilar to a high stakes TV game show. Strategically, Moses deferred to Aaron in this gambit, who turned his staff into a serpent before Pharaoh. The court magicians countered, but Aaron transcended magic. Theologian Martin Buber believed the profound barrier between magic and religion was key to protecting the sacred name God, at the burning bush, had given to Moses. Buber assailed Egypt for mistaking base sorcery for the sublime. The Coronavirus carried all the known attributes of the biblical plagues. At the height of our horrid summer viral spike, we heard the White House praise Houston's obscure Dr. Stella Immanuel who deplored sexual visitations by her demons causing gynecological defects while promising the supernatural effectiveness of hydroxychloroquine. I wondered how Buber would analyze these fucking quacks, carnival barkers and charlatans, while a world spun defenseless against a hurtling plague conjured in an Asian wet market.

There was an email from Yunmei late last night. Stamp mark showed 2:10am and the message was written like a poem in Apple Chancery font. She wanted very much to meet again before my flight back to California and offered to come by the airport if that made things easier. I didn't know how to process the request. My flight was late afternoon and the day had nothing pressing. It didn't seem right to have her airtrain to JFK but driving into upper Manhattan felt like too much work. I was intending to walk around the Roslyn duck pond and then Port Washington harbor to see the sail boats. There was a chance to catch an old high school friend Larry Miller too who was working from home in Westbury. All the vague plans made days before fell apart because of the growing dark mood enveloping me. I had doubted that seeing another person from the past would be an ascent and yet spending another day in isolation guaranteed no joy.

Over the buffet breakfast I read the newspaper on my iPad. With the mounting hacking into government and corporate accounts becoming the weekly norm, the ceiling overhead appeared quite shaky and destined to collapse. Adding to this the many instances of Zoom bombing pornography and racist tropes into our scheduled online classes, there was little left to reinvigorate the public trust. The coffee this morning was strong and braced me. I decided to drive into Manhattan to see Yunmei.

Getting Cassandra back into the cat carrier was daunting in preparation for checkout. Perhaps she had intuited that we were leaving the motel room and she went between the bed's headboard and night table. I had put out some catnip prior to breakfast but that didn't lessen her anxiety. Cassandra made ample use of the kitty box and she managed to spread litter over the carpet. However, I was relieved that she didn't urinate on the floor. Her bowel movements were colossal. After a few minutes, she came out from behind the headboard and I positioned her inside the cat carrier.

While checking out I phoned my son and daughter. I should have done that last night but I thought texting yesterday was sufficient. But neither teen last night had texted back. Barry picked up this morning. Ariel didn't. This was the norm. All was fine at home. Barry remembered to put out the trash and recycle bins. He was fine with frozen foods, pre-washed salad packages, and pizza.

With the car gassed up, I drove around the town of Roslyn and stopped briefly to walk a pleasing circuit around the lake. The maple trees were turning color. I left the car windows partly open. Yunmei was expecting me in two hours. The open-air walk should chase the doldrums away. The weather comfortable and sunny. There were energetic black ducks on parade.

I drove to Manhattan in moderate traffic on the Long Island Expressway. Cassandra was vocal in the front seat. I dared not let her out of the carrier. Benny warned me never to allow her loose inside a car, lest she urinate everywhere. I tried having a conversation with Cassandra since Benny claimed that language calmed her during moments of stress. I had been known to fail at small talk. Undaunted, I tried to tell her the history of ducks on Long Island. That was a non-starter. Then I proceeded to say everything I knew about Alain Resnais' misguided French masterpiece, *L'Année dernière à Marienbad*. I conveyed to Cassandra that the film introduced a beautiful woman and a handsome man inside a converted palace hotel. They walk and talk and walk going nowhere. They may have met the year before. They may have dreamt about an affair or they may have started a romance the previous year. They are certain of nothing. The film introduces a second man who may be her husband. Perhaps Cassandra found all of this summary fascinating. She ceased crying. I also translated the title for her comprehension: *Last Year at Marienbad*.

As there are some days in the year when I receive incredibly positive luck from the universe, I was able to find free street parking two blocks from Yunmei's apartment along Amsterdam Avenue. I left a crack in all four car door windows for the cat's benefit and texted her that I was three minutes away. Yunmei texted back an emoji of a woman doing cartwheels. I walked briskly like an ex-New Yorker upon

34

return. I bought a New York Times at a newsstand to enjoy the feel of the paper under my arm. I told the guy with the BLM hat at the stand to keep the change acknowledging my parking good fortune. Likewise, I was prepared to tip the pilot on my return flight if luck prevailed.

Yunmei was standing outside her apartment house when I arrived. She was wearing sweat pants, a Columbia sweat shirt, and a Mets baseball cap. I recognized a different pair of eyeglasses for her – these were gold rimmed and oval, larger than proportional to her angular face. She had on a cloth face mask. I forgot to get out my N95.

"Hi professor."

"Hi Yunmei. I'm legally parked but I have a cat in the car."

"Oh. A cat?"

"It was a gift. I think I'm good for an hour."

"Do you like cats?"

"No, actually I don't."

"That's a strange gift, professor."

"Yes."

"I'll take the cat for you." she said openly. "I'm good with cats."

I explained indelicately that the cat was a contractual arrangement that can be interpreted as a present that cannot be regifted. This went beyond gifting etiquette. I told her that I would be flying to California with the cat and taking photos of the cat for many months to come to please the original owner. Yunmei knitted her wispy eyebrows. She suggested that we walk to Morningside Park as I fumbled for my mask inside my jacket pocket.

Her fall semester classes had begun and she had some hybrid classes to protect her matriculation and visa status as an international student. She also had one online course on film theory. Columbia had advised all international students to live on or close to campus. Yunmei added that there was a great amount of confusion at Columbia on the last-minute changes of course offerings and the trend to convert in-person courses to remote courses. I told her that I only had one cinema course to teach remotely this fall on Zoom. It was a fantasy genre class which she had taken with me two years ago.

"What are you writing?" she asked.

35

"A study on the visual confluence, fantasy, and wit of Jean-Pierre Jeunet and Terry Gilliam. Film director as trickster."

"Cool. Fantasia cinema. They'll appreciate a book like that."

"Maybe the film community will." I said.

"*Brazil* would have been pure genius if he had cut it down to 99 minutes."

That made me laugh.

"You look like the *Brazil* character Sam Lowry."

"Do I really?"

"Yes. Sad eyes as the world turns sour."

"Gilliam always goes too long. While Jeunet's *Amélie* is perfect at 2 hours."

We halted at the corner of 121st Street and Morningside Drive watching skateboarders crash into an expensive Trek bicycle. The collision could have been comic had tempers not been so hot. The incident was at risk of becoming a racial conflict. We crossed Morningside rapidly and entered the park. A NYPD car was cruising uptown.

"Do you prefer Gilliam to Jeunet?"

I didn't have a good answer.

"Despite his penchant for going long, I prefer Gilliam." Yunmei said "He is more autobiographical, perverse, and paranoid like a coke addict. Yet the French are totally fucked up."

"Why do you say that?"

"The French think they invented civilization."

"Didn't they?" I threw this back at her for sport.

"They invented attitude. That's not civilization."

She projected an intense countenance that was her signature.

"My parents want me home. My mother thinks the United States can't manage the COVID crisis based on the insane U.S. death toll and Trump's stupidity. I might have to go back in January. She blames your country for gross negligence."

"Your mother's correct."

"She warned me about studying here. But I didn't want to go to England. I'm on a full scholarship so if I can just get a nanny job I can tell my mother to back off. China is still fighting the virus, even with a strong, central plan."

"It's not legal for you to work here, Yunmei."

"Others do it off the books. New York is expensive."

"You like New York that much?"

"I love New York. It never sleeps. I've insomnia but the city forgives this sickness. The museums will open eventually. When I was a girl, I had an imaginary friend Yoyo. And the other day, Yoyo came back into my life. She talks to me when I wake. I think I'm going into my second childhood. Ha, ha."

The conversation lapsed. We walked for awhile quietly. New York was once the epicenter of the pandemic in America. Now the city and the state were moving forward while the rest of the country, especially California, was overwhelmed by the daily mortality rate. Much of America was arguing with itself about whether to don a mask or to dismiss the virus as a political hoax.

"I liked office hours with you, professor. I remember each and every conversation. You would take me out of myself. I felt understood. You emit blue light. You make me think about why I want to live, to make film art, to make a life in art. If I spend too much time alone, it's not good. I shrink like Alice in Wonderland. I get so small. I hate the bathroom mirror. My father could be the Mad Hatter. When I don't talk to you, I lose my place. I forget to smile. Growing up, I was never given toys. Do you know what I mean?"

"I'm trying to follow you, Yunmei. I think I know what you're saying."

"Try harder, professor."

The park had a lot of activity. The wind was refreshing. Removing my mask for a moment, the air quality seemed good. She removed her N95 too. I noticed her pink lip gloss.

"Charlie Chaplin or Buster Keaton?" Yunmei asked in a non sequitur.

"Who would make the better nanny?"

"Who talks to you in silent screen?"

"When I was twenty I liked Chaplin. Now I like Keaton."

37

"In twenty years you'll go back to Chaplin." she said like a Tarot card reader.

"Chaplin was sentimental."

"What's bad about sentimental?" she asked coolly.

"Nothing in life. Everything in art. This is about taste. Renoir or Cezanne. I once preferred Renoir but now Cezanne. Keaton's cerebral and saw human motion from God's eye. Keaton embodied the best of Spinoza and Wittgenstein."

"Who's Wittgenstein?"

I clarified why I referenced Wittgenstein which seemed to annoy her. Maybe she was tired of being outside. On the occasions when I mention and define Wittgenstein I seem to piss people off. She put her face mask back on.

"Beckett made a short film with Keaton. In the 1960s."

"Yes. Directed by Alan Schneider. Beckett wrote the script." I said.

My mind left the conversation and reverted to Cassandra in the rental car. It was as though I was sensing the cat's distress. I tugged at my face mask. I knew the Beckett film and was respectful of its existence. However, the concoction was not much more adept than a graduate student homage to Luis Buñuel.

"I think Beckett wanted Chaplin to do the film but the script never got to Chaplin."

"Was Chaplin Jewish?" she asked.

"No."

"You know that the FBI thought Chaplin was a Communist born in France under the name Israel Thornstein?"

"I didn't know that. Is that on some Facebook page?"

"I don't use FB. FB sucks." Yunmei said as she played with her hair. "Didn't he make *The Great Dictator* because he was born Jewish?"

"He's not Jewish."

"Are you certain?"

"No."

"Do you want to make a bet?"

"If I bet, I'll lose two dollars."

She laughed.

"Did you know that Alan Schneider taught theatre in San Diego in the 1980s?"

"You're Jewish."

"Yes."

"Is it a sin for a Jew to commit suicide?"

"I really don't know. I think the Jewish religion forbids it. Why do you ask?"

"There are sins. All major religions have sins."

"Yes." I said.

"Chinese Buddhism's first precept prohibits all aspects of killing, both humans and all animals. Scholars interpret Buddhist texts about the precepts as an opposition to capital punishment, suicide, abortion, euthanasia."

"I know that, Yunmei."

"I tried to take my life when I was fifteen. I was overwhelmed by anger. I had to be hospitalized. I cut my wrist."

"Oh God…"

"You told the large film class in the winter of 2019 that you're Jewish, and life was like a short sentence that ends with a question mark."

"Maybe that was a punchline to a joke."

"I didn't get the joke." Yunmei replied.

"Sometimes I ad-lib."

"What is ad-lib?"

"Extemporize."

"Why did Chaplin marry a girl who was just eighteen?"

"I don't know, Yunmei. He had to be triple her age."

"You look uncomfortable, professor."

"I'm thinking the cops will ticket me for having a cat locked inside."

Yunmei laughed quietly. She found this cat business funny. Just ahead were three dogs chasing some rodent. Yunmei informed me that she usually didn't go into Morningside Heights park alone. She became aware that the few times she explored Manhattan parks by herself she was flooded with surging panic attacks. She politely inquired when I would share the book chapters on Jeunet and Gilliam with her. I said that I don't reveal drafts until they are ready for galley proofs.

We reversed direction and headed back to her apartment building. There were two more police cars circling the block opposite the park. Yunmei thanked me for visiting and for allowing so many emails to flow between us. She expressed appreciation that few of her teachers ever cared about her artwork, her health, her family difficulties, and problems fitting into any academic community.

"You must be a good father to your children."

"Thank you."

"My father is built out of steel. Not you. You have flesh."

"I have some steel, Yunmei."

The conversation was coming to an end. It was getting serious and intuitive. Yunmei tipped her N95 mask below her nose and lips. A delicate smile surfaced. She stood statuesque, her mask rose over her nose, and then Yunmei stepped forward to hug me. I returned the hug, our masks tightly over our ears and careful that our heads did not collide.

CHAPTER SIX

I arrived at check-in an extra hour sooner to ensure Cassandra's booking on American Airlines to San Diego. It helped to have extra time since I was flying on a mileage award that included business class each way but unpaid seats were never completely reliable. New York airport crowds were not a reality this year. Jet travel in 2020 was an immersion into dystopian movies and novels about an intergalactic disaster. The public service announcements over the airport intercom had embroidered the post 9/11 era warnings about not accepting packages from strangers with reminders that facial covering and social distancing requirements are in effect. In my private consciousness I weighed the statistical chances of an act of terrorism compared to the probability of getting Coronavirus on the westbound journey. I had antibodies for one of these two absurd prongs.

The airline was fine with the official cat carrier case and Cassandra's weight was within American's pet chart. Perhaps most fortunate, the cat was not caterwauling to be a total nuisance. By talking to her in a whisper, I had tranquilized the animal per Benny's prescriptions. Apparently business class permitted two pets per flight compared to five pets in the coach section. There was an extravagant cash surcharge for my precious cargo which helped American cope with the economic tanking of the airline industry. Luckily, this was a non-stop flight and I placed the rest of the catnip inside the carrier. TSA thought it was marijuana but I had the pet store packaging in my jacket pocket.

After drinking a glass of merlot after takeoff, I decided not to watch an onboard movie and to try to doze off or lose myself with an eBook.

My choices were the self-righteous John Bolton tome that pissed off the Trump administration, Woody Allen's self-congratulatory memoir which ignited his estranged son Rowan Farrow – both eBooks from the public lending library – and an illegal copy of Mary Trump's *Too Much and Never Enough*. One of my graduate students had frequented the dark web and sent me a virus-free, pirated Mary Trump PDF. I tried a dozen pages from each book feeling very unsatisfied. All the tedious writing struck me as American cultural wallpaper. I then found in my iPad Graham Greene's *The Power and The Glory* which I had read decades ago and had loved Greene's dignity imposed on a damaged, sympathetic member of clergy. Like many of Greene's stories that skirt strict Catholicism, he injected a complex empathy within a renegade 'whisky priest' from the Mexican state of Tabasco. I thought the priest was heroic. It was a fast, spiritual, and comforting read.

My seat companion was a stout, natty businessman who had a plastic face shield riding above his N95. He said his name was Reginald. I nicknamed him Ralph. He looked like he managed five hundred employees in seven rust belt cities. He had tried to move to another seat when his eyes spotted the cat carrier. Business class was at capacity. He stopped short of bribing the on-board convivial attendant while fumbling for his wallet. If Ralph were Benny, the bribe would have been executed miraculously. Ralph was stuck with me, while I had Graham Greene at his best.

What's so encompassing about Greene's Mexican tale is the graceful arc of the Catholic priest's escape into a neighboring province from a relentless, morally irreproachable lieutenant and posse, only to reunite with the Mestizo Indian who may be laying a trap for the priest to earn a bounty. The Mestizo convinces the vulnerable priest to hear the confession of a dying man and is compelled to follow priestly duty. Of course, the flawed priest gets caught and this fatalism is Greene territory. On the eve of the execution, the dispassionate lieutenant shows mercy with a twist in the story. Graham Greene has inhabited the priest's life totally as his alter ego, freeing the character of any extraneous intellectualism, materialism, and modern vanity.

Some years ago one of my rabbis told a loopy anecdote during a

Rosh Hashanah sermon. He had recalled a strange story told to him by a friend who habitually jogged inside Los Angeles' Griffith Park – a park at the eastern end of the Santa Monica Mountains. The season was either spring or autumn; I forgot that detail. The rabbi's friend – a woman in her late 40's – was jogging early in the morning. A black suv in her circular route was coming closer to her. She sped up all the while the vehicle continued to pursue her. When the suv was a few feet away, the male driver lowered his window and said he required help. His suv then came to a stop. The jogger made a split-second decision to go against her defense instinct since the driver appeared in shock or medically unwell.

The driver said to the woman that he had inadvertently hit a small deer and didn't know what to do. He didn't have his cell phone with him. The jogger had her phone and offered to call for help. She asked him the location of the fallen deer. The driver told her that he feared leaving the deer by the road and therefore he put the animal inside the suv. The jogger was leery and thoroughly uncomfortable with the situation. The driver, standing behind his vehicle, suddenly opened the hatch with his key fob. Inside was the deer supine, which startled the jogger. She found the image too bizarre. In the next instant, the deer awoke and bolted out of the car. My rabbi had identified this moment as an existential revelation for the deer and for the two witnesses. The deer was given back life. The jogger and the driver, according to my rabbi, learned half of the deer's lesson and could spend the rest of their lives learning the other half.

I asked my rabbi if this was a real anecdote and he smiled. He said it was probably 99% true. That was that. I didn't challenge the remark. To this day I am unclear why he didn't say it was 100%. Many rabbis apply a vague memory regarding anecdotal names as anonymity being one of the oldest foundation of all spiritual traditions.

The spinning coin of my own belief system depicted one side Judaism and the flip side agnosticism. I preferred Judaism. Judaism warded off loneliness. This proclivity was embedded in my lineage as all my known ancestors were Jewish. The life of French philosopher Simone Weil embodied a more paradoxical duality as she was born a Jew but nearly died a Catholic. She, like so many European Jews, suffered greatly under the sadistic shadow of Hitler. She resented her sex, her bourgeois privilege, and her Jewish roots. She loved the downtrodden, philosophical books and cigarettes. She died the same age as Christ. Weil's writings had moved me when I was young as did the books by Thomas Merton. Catholics, fearing hell, know in their bones hell exists but Jews don't give a fuck. This was why I always liked Graham Greene.

I left my seat for the plane's lavatory. In the cramped space framed by the mirror over the sink, my face aged. The N95 around my chin, I spotted harsh vertical lines south of my mouth. My darkened eyes squinted. They were the beaten, wizened eyes of Clint Eastwood in *Gran Torino.* I read that faces distort over long air travel. Jet cabins can reach 20 percent humidity. Skin is comfortable between 40 to 70 percent humidity. Lack of humidity dehydrates skin. Flights pressurized between 6,000 to 8,000 feet, equivalent to a mountain top. Less blood flow to skin can make the face ashen. The phenomenology of one's face in transformation, advancing age and character, can never approximate Oscar Wilde's *The Portrait of Dorian Gray.*

My disdainful flight companion Ralph seemed put upon when I returned to my seat. Nonetheless, I smiled and said something pleasant about NASDAQ. Getting no reaction, I promised him that I would pay for his taxi after we landed. He wouldn't take my university business card. Cassandra was crying in a delicate, soft rhythm. I slipped one finger through the cat carrier's air hole to soothe her. I received a tender bite.

"Cats have nine lives. She's on number eight." I said to Ralph who noticed I got bit.

He didn't laugh. So I did.

My mind was drifting towards my daughter Ariel. I missed her younger self. She loved cats. She loved art projects on the kitchen table and outside on the patio. She made gigantic papier mâché animals which were painted with primary color acrylics. Ariel named each creation and kept them in a magic zoo. My mind then drifted to Benny

Edelmann. He seemed to be a dog guy. That particular person who would keep a large barking hound in the backyard until midnight. Not just any dog. A Doberman. A Rottweiler. An Akita. Any large breed but Scooby-Doo. I couldn't figure out why he didn't hunt a little harder for an assisted living facility with pet friendly rules.

My father had regaled me with several classic Benny stories when the two men flew VIP to Las Vegas in the late 1970s. My Dad liked old Vegas before the town became a family destination with Cirque du Soleil's *Mystère* in the early '90s. Dad never witnessed the city's makeover. At the Golden Nugget Hotel, Benny was usually an albatross around my father's neck. The Golden Nugget loved to shower Benny with free junkets and escorts. Edelmann was a fanatical craps player who tanked every other junket, but sometimes made a killing. Consequently these sojourns with Benny were complimentary from the big three Vegas hotels at the time. When not provided escorts, he picked up stray anorexic women at the bar. He tried to convince my father that anorexia prevented pregnancies and venereal disease. Further, redheads under one hundred pounds guaranteed Benny marvelous gambling outcomes and no guilt trips. Once, my father was playing a hundred-dollar craps table at Caesar's Palace where Benny imagined had the greatest concentration of redheads. Benny joined him an hour later having finally found a rail-thin, redhead to hang with him. She was actually a cross between Meg Ryan and Sinéad O'Connor, assuming I got the description accurate.

At the craps table, Benny and the woman began kissing with abandon. Benny, overconfident and over-aroused, took a marker for one hundred thousand dollars and played twentyfive thousand on the pass line with full odds. He had a come bet every roll – again with full odds. My father had the dice and rolled for about half an hour. Benny cashed out for just over a quarter of a million and directed the woman to work her magic on my father while nudging him to jump to the big roller table. My father balked and stayed put, losing ten grand that evening. In 1978 that was a costly setback. Benny covered his loss that weekend.

Some junkets, Benny brought along his wife Joan to preserve his marriage. My father sat out those trips. Benny's wife was a kleptomaniac with a penchant for packing hotel terry robes, slippers, branded towels and shot glasses in her luggage when checking out. Benny made certain to pay the front desk for the missing accessories every visit to preserve his VIP junket status and avoiding embarrassment in the lobby at checkout. My father said there was a linen closet in Benny's home that was crammed with hotel brand paraphernalia which he kept under lock and key. Benny didn't want the house maid ever to see the stash. There was a mean rumor that Joan was dressed in a hotel robe in her coffin to meet her specific wishes, but the casket was closed during her memorial fortunately.

Benny earned a special place in our complicated family history and this fact should really disturb me more. Benny knew that my father had lobbied me for years while I was in high school, in college, and in grad school. My father was determined to insert me into his car business. My father had cast me as his understudy and heir apparent. After all, the business was rocketing to remarkable profitability, becoming a top dealership on the North Shore. Selling was a powerful art, which my father believed was our major family trait. According to my father, America was built on the backs of great salesmen. The gifted broker will always make a conquest because he never hears the word "no". The American salesman is mortal but eternal, according to my father. But to Benny, the devil was the world's best salesman. Benny believed my father was the most unorthodox sales talent of the last century. Nonetheless, Benny persuaded my old man to give me freedom to pursue an academic career. Benny scouted me as an introverted, nervous intellectual – a poor fit to push new cars and managing sales staff. I watched them argue about it over many evenings. Two Jews from the World War II generation in fierce debate which should have been taped for posterity – as scintillating as bellicose Borsch Belt dining room fights. Benny's madcap wife once told me that Benny made a deciding difference in this affair. Joan was correct. My father gave up the battle with me.

When the plane came in for a landing over the San Diego skyline,

Ralph had out his oversized phone. Cassandra took the air pressure change badly, wailing. We deplaned in a flash. This was an uncomfortable flight but, with a high strung cat, the travel might have been ten times worse. At baggage claim, I grabbed my suitcase and summoned a Lyft. My phone rang. It was Celeste and I took the call outside the terminal.

"I miss you."

"I miss you too."

"How was your flight?"

"Okay."

"It was good to see you."

"Great to see you, Celeste. It's got to be late in New York."

"Past midnight. You're on my mind."

"I could use some sleep and deal with jet lag. I have to teach tomorrow."

"You'll be kickass good. You know these lectures by heart."

"Yeah. I need to text my kids that I arrived."

"Are they picking you up?"

"No."

Her breathing was a little heavy.

"I have to tell you something, Jonathan."

"Okay."

"I should have said this at the restaurant."

We both fell silent.

"What, Celeste? My Lyft is coming in a few minutes."

"At the time we broke up and I was furious at you...and your tenure obsession."

Silence again.

"There was a month that went by and you were travelling...and I decided to have an abortion."

A very long silence.

"I should have told you when I moved out of your apartment, Jonathan. It took years to face this crap and don't hate me tonight for harboring secrets."

"Celeste."

"You must have known, Jonathan. Men know."

"I didn't know."

"You know my inner thoughts."

"Celeste."

The cell phone call dropped. Or she hung up.

CHAPTER SEVEN

Saturday morning I got up inside my own bedroom but it felt like a stranger's home. I was uncomfortable about things despite the recognizable elements of the house. There was a slight odor of mildew. The shades were not down completely and the sun was strong around eight in the morning. The sound of crows was audible. We seldom hear crows in this neighborhood and I never liked hearing them any time of day. A murder of crows. Sunday evening would be the start of Yom Kippur. My son Barry was sleeping late. His sister Ariel apparently was not around for the weekend and I could glean that something half devious was in the making. She was supposed to share responsibilities with Barry during my six days away. One hundred and forty-four hours. Neither one was the house cook but together they were to be a little safer and wiser without a parent. There would be another person who can drive in an emergency. Some parents would never leave teens alone, but of course this question is contoured on teen maturity and on the parents' sense of trust. Never would I travel for two weeks under this arrangement. Less than a week was a realistic window. My immediate neighbors, in the large asymmetrical Spanish stucco house on the left, knew I was away and I relied on their discreet eyes and ears. The gregarious, married couple next door on our right would only text if something horrid was detectable from the telltale cars parked along our street. They were from Iran and both were practicing dentists, had adorable twin preschool children and a copper colored Goldendoodle larger than a llama. Once they had informed me on the Fourth of July that they found a baby rattlesnake in their backyard during their barbeque and asked me to find an empty box to help capture it. Everything reciprocal proved we are sentient, social yet scared souls.

"Hey Dad, can I have breakfast?"

This was shouted across the hall. I also heard the cat meowing from the spare bedroom converted into a home office. Entering Barry's room after knocking, I saw all of his laundry scattered along the carpet and several empty crushed cans of soda on his book shelf. It looked like a stage set on the theme of teenage order. He was under a blanket, his bare legs exposed but no sign of a head. His feet appeared larger than ever.

"Good morning."

"Could you make an omelet?"

"I could."

I uttered the obnoxious prompt and got the right response.

"Please."

"Thank you."

"There's no bacon unless you hid some in the freezer."

"There's always bacon on the freezer slider shelf."

"Yeah."

"How was school?"

"Online sucks. We're out of toilet paper."

"There's a ton of toilet paper in the garage."

"Oh. Fuck it. I hate looking for crap in the garage."

Barry had worked hard containing his newly acquired vocabulary of an eighteen-wheel truck driver. He wasn't embarrassed about his issue about going alone into our garage and his phobia about arachnids which we had in abundance. Barry couldn't kill a spider with his shoe or a Louisville Slugger baseball bat. I pulled the quilt below his head and he shot me a look of ambivalence mixed with entitlement. These were the moments when I was uncertain whether I was a failed father or an underpaid valet. I had no doubt that Barry had courage about many things and that he also loved me. I suspected that if I hadn't become a college professor at a university I would have eventually found my calling inside a rambling mansion tending to a sibilant, bald land baron suffering chronic hip bursitis. My fluffy egg white omelets were as accomplished as a three-star Michelin chef. It's how you whip the eggs and sneak in thyme.

"Where's Ariel?"

"I don't know."

"When did you see her last?"

"Maybe three days ago?"

"Is she okay?"

"I don't know. Call her."

"Ariel was supposed to stay with you."

"I know."

We both could hear the cat during this exchange.

"Did you bring back a fucking cat?"

"Yes."

"Why?"

"I know a gangster absent a neck, Barry. A friend of grandpa. And I'm doing a favor. This is temporary."

Barry had a way of laughing which wasn't noticeably loud but wasn't kind. Teens had perfected this swallowed sound to undermine context, while faking rapport. Whenever I attempted to imitate this laugh, Barry would call me on it.

"You'll like this cat, Barry."

"A cat? I'm not cleaning litter boxes. And they spray on everything even after you fix them."

"This cat isn't male."

I left his room. I heard Cassandra in her new octave range. I walked to my daughter's room. Ariel's bed was unmade, her bay window was wide open, an empty pack of cigarettes was on her night stand, several stuffed animals were strewn at the foot of the bed, shoes and fashion boots were tossed about, cut flowers were wilting in a small ceramic vase. A surfer's photo was taped on the cork board and torn pages from magazines messed the corner. I did not like this surfer, whether or not he was local or from the internet. I heard more loud crows outside.

Inside Ariel's bedroom, sensations and time raced through me. She was a kindergarten girl playing with talking stuffed animals inside this room. Our family had acquired a half dozen American Girl dolls on eBay in a buying frenzy beginning with her seventh birthday. We weren't permitted to toss away the accompanying brand boxes for each doll. She loved the fancy containers and they were stored meticulously in the suspended metal storage unit under the garage ceiling. Ariel's sliding closet doors were off the guiding tracks, conveying a look of an earthquake. Ariel's enduring complaint since early teens years to me – the mismatched closet doors ate her hanging clothes and bit her fingers.

I made Barry his three-egg omelet in our kitchen downstairs and texted him that breakfast was on the table. I had skipped my own breakfast and relied on Café Bustelo Cuban roast black coffee. No milk. No sugar. He texted back: *thx.coming now.*

The next breakfast was Cassandra's. She stopped crying after the kibble was poured into the feed bowl. For the first time, the cat rubbed her body against my pajama leg which caused a slight frisson. Experiencing the cat in my own home nudged me into an epiphany about Cassandra's next home. I would find a graduate student who needed an annuity and the student would be the foster address for Cassandra. She will be cared, honoring the pledge to Benny. I'll visit the cat for the evidentiary photos, but also ask the student to take photos to send me. This was the perfect solution. Benny will never know.

I shuffled peacefully through the living room and the den. There were many family photos. Traci looked fabulous and alive in each frame. Her presence lingered in every square inch of space. I took my coffee to the fenced patio while the cat began to purr and sat on a metal lawn chair. I didn't want to think about Ariel's whereabouts just yet. In the days ahead there would be meditation during Yom Kippur. During the High Holy Days I expected to examine where family was heading. I could process the feelings for Celeste and also her news over the phone. I couldn't comprehend why Celeste withheld her abortion from me for so long.

Self-flagellation was one of my old habits and with this disorder, "Schrödinger's cat" snuck into my consciousness. Quantum physicists had applied the Schrödinger's cat concept for several complex theoretical purposes. As I understand it, a cat is placed in a sealed container with a radioactive element and a poison that will be released if an atom of the radioactive substance decays. The superposition theorem posits that a phenomenon can only be analyzed with only one source of power at a time. Quantum physics suggests that until somebody opens the container, the cat is both alive and dead, a superposition of states. Opening the container to witness the cat causes it to change its quantum state randomly, forcing it to be either alive or dead. Therefore, I was closer to being a near perfect model of Schrödinger's cat than Cassandra. All my internal emotions told me that I was either alive or dead. There, for each mortal soul, exists a moment when we might have perished and still apprehend a clear, dark signal. A moment of afterlife without a body, without an identity, without a destination. This was how I felt when Traci died and this was my state of being this awful year.

On the patio I heard a leaf blower in the distance. A jet flew overhead. No more sounds of crows. I was barefoot on cool ceramic patio tile. My cell phone, on the patio table, rang. I guessed that it was Ariel but the call was from Oscar Gerhardt, a faculty friend from campus. He phoned me regularly, never texting. I probably liked that. Oscar Gerhardt was tenured in the Literature Department. He was a few years younger but carried himself like my elder brother. Last summer he wore a cowboy hat and stopped shaving. He thought he could pass as a less handsome Garth Brooks. I answered the phone.

"Oscar..."

"Hey, are you back?"

"Got in last night. Exhausted."

"How was it?"

"Okay."

"You couldn't get me on a plane if you paid me a million dollars."

"I have COVID antibodies."

"You're still a moron for flying."

The call was not timed well. His calls go longer than an hour.

"How's your father?"

"Off the ventilator. The hospital will release him in a week."

"That's great news, Oscar."

"Fucking Asian virus."

"Can I call you tomorrow? This isn't a convenient time."

"Tomorrow's not good. I won't be long."

"What's up?"

"The faculty vote is scheduled for Monday."

"Okay."

"Will you be in the Zoom meeting?"

"No, it's Yom Kippur."

"Well, how stupid is that. Who scheduled this Zoom?" Gerhardt snorted.

"The department chair."

"Isn't Horowitz Jewish?"

"Yeah, he is."

"So why's he such an asshole?"

"He's not a practicing Jew." I replied. "He's a cross between a Misotheist and a Scientologist."

Gerhardt bellowed. His laugh sounded like a goat's fart.

"A Misotheist believes that God exists but doesn't always do good and often does evil?"

"No, that's a Dystheist." I said. "A Misotheist simply hates God whatever the hell God is doing."

"You don't like Horowitz?"

"I like Horowitz enough."

"What the fuck does that mean?"

"Horowitz is a weather vane."

"Like the Dylan tune 'Subterranean Homesick Blues'…"

I knew the lyrics about which way the wind blows.

Gerhardt adjusted his tone.

"I need a big favor, Jonathan."

"What?"

"I don't ask for favors. I don't abuse my close friends. You know I always tell things truthfully. Particularly to you. One of my graduate students lodged a formal complaint and I need a witness."

"A witness for what?"

"That she was flirting with me many times at the faculty club last year and I asked for boundaries."

"Oh Christ, Oscar."

"You know the student. You know she baits older men. You were at the table."

"I don't know the student and I don't recall seeing anything."

"It's Brenda Whitaker, Jonathan. With the tiny mole at the edge of her brow. She's very attractive. You had her in one of your seminars too."

"I know her. She doesn't flirt with faculty."

"She does. She did with me. You were there.

CHAPTER EIGHT

Gerhardt was downplaying his worry. A formal charge could very well lead to his dismissal, tenure or no tenure. At age sixty, this would be the ending of his university career. He had a similar complication in 2015 which he skated through using some agility and dumb luck. Our senior colleagues in Lit, Edgar Whitehead and Dolores Bridges, went to bat for him with regard to a postdoc having teaching duties for our department. There was a messy internal department review and an inquiry from the campus office on sexual harassment. The internal review managed to quiet the postdoc and her complaint with better teaching assignments. Gerhardt got by with a formal warning landing in his academic file and preparing a formal written apology to the postdoc. Luck comes and luck goes. Those who knew Gerhardt quite well speculated that his karma sank while golfing drunk at Torrey Pines when his one wood shot killed a baby seagull on the eighteenth hole. Gerhardt when inebriated would tell his party company that in the late 1970s he slept with Stevie Nicks from Fleetwood Mac, having attended one of the VIP backstage parties for the band. He blamed his bad fortunes over forty years on Stevie Nicks who – according to Gerhardt – gave him a sexually transmitted disease that was late in proper treatment.

My perception of him during that 2015 campus intimacy inquiry was mixed. Gerhardt was happily married to his high school sweetheart. He always told us that fact. Looking within his campus office one would see numerous upbeat family photos. His wife privately might have reached her threshold with his drinking problem, but publically they were very unified and caring to one another. He had received a Fulbright and several Guggenheim fellowships. Yes, his conversations over one too many drinks betrayed dignity, unmasking his libido and adolescent bravado. Many colleagues had judged him as a clever joker with a streak of cowardice. Sober, he knew better than to compromise himself, abuse a student's trust, and hurt our department with harassment charges. One of his handy rationalizations for transgressing best practices was during his year teaching in Madrid on an exchange program. Gerhardt praised the public Spanish university for open freedoms between faculty and graduate students. At least that was his interpretation a dozen years ago. He thought a Catholic nation had an edge on America. At the same time, he never bragged about an affair with any student in Spain. But I suspected there was one young woman – Luciana – he had worshipped every week he was there.

As to Brenda Whitaker, I knew her not well but more than in a superficial manner. She was smart, attractive, well dressed, with genuine reserve, in her third year towards her doctorate. Faculty respected her high diligence, her many prestigious conferences around the country, and her serious mien. I couldn't say that Brenda ever breached boundaries. The notion was ludicrous. I truly doubted whatever Gerhardt was projecting onto her. Sometimes his lying would overwhelm his own memory. I would take Brenda's word over Gerhardt's. Therefore, I couldn't be a witness or an ally for him. Even if she were inappropriate with him at an afterhours event, that cannot be the justification for him to cross a line. Gerhardt, hearing my decision repeated again as final, wouldn't prevent him from begging with his entire life. Certainly, Dolores and Edgar wouldn't risk their respective reputations on his behalf a second time.

Jason Horowitz never liked Gerhardt and it became more apparent when Horowitz entered into the role of chair. Horowitz was born tightly wound, unctuous, and mannered like a handful of claustrophobic OCD people. Of course, Gerhardt occupied the opposite spectrum of personality types. These two tended to argue with one another during long, unforgiving faculty meetings. Horowitz resented peer colleagues who were breezy, casual, and lacking academic fastidiousness.

Paradoxically both men were equally pegged by junior faculty as smug, supercilious and strident. No fan club for these two men. I had befriended Gerhardt upon our initial meetings as we were the incoming generation of new hires eons ago, but I never grew close to Horowitz. So Gerhardt landed into the perfect fly trap and he was a victim of his own denial. There were many notable qualities to Gerhardt, particularly during his first decade teaching here. Gerhardt won a coveted campus-wide educator award and found large grant money for his doctoral students. When Gerhardt was promoted to Associate Professor, the Washington Post did a flattering feature on him as a leading national scholar on the evolving graphic novel and his caustic reconsideration of Art Spiegelman's *Maus* series. For years, he elevated his students and granted the hardest working students unlimited access to his constellation of authorities, teaching opportunities, and academic presses. When his better angels prevailed, Gerhardt was a noble, generous man.

Horowitz, like me, originated from New York but he was never a scrappy city kid. Far from it, Horowitz was led by the evening star of entitlement. He was born with a platinum stick up his rectum. To crystalize this, not only did he look uncannily like Trump's ghostly pale son-in-law Jared Kushner, but Horowitz held most of Kushner's celebrated, self-satisfied traits. Horowitz came from wealth within the elite Connecticut real estate world plus family holdings in the Colt gun company based in Hartford. He had Kushner's buoying boyish features – the lanky reed build, and that silly adenoidal tone of a kiss-ass choir lad. Horowitz was blessed doubly, married to an affluent blonde beauty, Lexy Ford, who spent a quarter of her life enhancing or correcting La Jolla facelifts. Department Chair Horowitz was a master of obsequious gestures to his campus overlords all the way up to the Chancellor. Unlike Kushner who reportedly was an observant orthodox Jew, Horowitz distanced himself from most things culturally Jewish but he used his Jewish surname, his family background, along with his knowledge of Irving Howe and Bernard Malamud when convenient in fundraising goals.

Jason Horowitz's ties to his father-in-law who was Associate Chancellor Charles Vincent Ford, like Jared Kushner's ties to Trump, paralleled farcically the tale of Charlemagne, the eighth century King of the Franks. Fabled Charlemagne had many reasons to wed his attractive daughter to a stellar court Jew. Key among the many incentives for Charlemagne was that a Jewish son-in-law secured the affection of the considerable affluent Jews in his Kingdom. That might have been true for entrepreneur Donald J. Trump in his swamp kingdom but less so for the Chancellor's office.

Horowitz's charming wife was introduced to everyone in the department as Lexington Ford Horowitz which sounded like car dealership in Orange County, but over time senior faculty and Horowitz's inner circle were permitted to call her Lexy in her powder blue Lexus. Her vanity license plate was LXYLXS with a heart icon. Horowitz's wife had a habit of phoning Traci frequently for movie dates a week in advance, always choosing the film, and treating Traci to the movie. Traci seldom blew her off. Lexy liked that Traci came from Irish heritage and regaled Traci with Lexy's own Irish family stories. Lexy told my wife that she admired how Traci drove a manual transmission like Mario Andretti. That was one of Traci's special skills behind the wheel. Lexy enjoyed hot room yoga with Traci during the winter. I finished my coffee on the patio and began a short email letter to New Montefiore Cemetery requesting the staff inspect my parents' grave sites. I included my cell phone photos. The cemetery staff would wait until the High Holy Days were concluded before getting back to me. They were known to have a respectable supervising staff and I was willing to give them the benefit of the doubt about any negligence from their unionized ground crew.

COVID may not have changed the business of cemeteries and funerals adversely – the cascading death tolls added to graves everywhere – but certainly colleges and universities in all fifty states were struggling with the tragic budgetary shortfall. Dorms and residential life buildings were effectively vacant. That critical lost income plus lost cafeteria revenue, lost student and staff parking fees, and growing deferred admissions were the stuff of nightmares for administrators. Students from coast to coast were demanding breaks in tuition because of deficient Zoom and Canvas learning systems. Too many school administrations were misleading current and incoming students last June about a physical return to campus this fall term. Higher education was practicing its own swift hand at grifting.

The crisis was convenient for Ariel's extended gap year after high school. I always thought that she would excel at an art college that relaxed general education requirements. She had a superlative talent in high school freestyle drawing, video vine creation, pairing pop music with kinetic body movement on TikTok. I've relayed as much to her all through her junior and senior years. However, her view of life was like a mayfly which is to say that mayflies live only a day. She, like her friends, had little fear of COVID while my days entering April 2020 were filled with existential dread that my family and I would contract the virus and that I might even require a ventilator.

When Traci died, Ariel became a different soul. Within months she used a fraudulent ID and got a prominent tattoo on her ankle. Three other body artistries followed including a tramp stamp an inch over her butt. Minors need parental written consent to obtain a tattoo or body piercing. It's not that I despise skin graphics but when I see any human with fifteen inkings at the supermarket, I wish for eyeglasses with magic filters. Ariel was once an innocent girl who studied for a bat mitzvah and opted for a trip to Israel before turning thirteen. As a preteen, she never tried to speed her aging process. We did wholesome things that were supposed to yield long term dividends. I had to accept Ariel's rogue behavior as a natural counterforce to losing her mother. I had asked Barry repeatedly what was making his sister drift away but each response from him was something of a Zen koan. He murmured that kids can get bitch hard and twist their world until they bleed. Ariel was getting stranger to Barry, and yet he respected her need for a wilder freedom, even if it was simply a carousel of joy and pain. Would Traci have handled this more successfully had I been the parent to fall to cancer? Would the two of us see this version of Ariel in 2020?

My phone rang. It was Benny Edelmann. I hesitated.

"Hello Benny."

"Hello Jonathan."

"You beat me to it. I was about to call."

"I didn't get any photos."

"My carrier is T-Mobile. They're awful, Benny. I sent you hours ago two photos of the cat."

"You're back in California?"

"Yeah."

"Send them again. Now. While I'm on the phone."

I got up, left the patio, and went to find Benny's cat. Cassandra was under the bed.

"Benny, you still there?"

"Yeah, I'm still here."

"Give me two seconds, okay?"

On my knees I reached for Cassandra. She nearly bit me. I placed her on the window sill overlooking the patio's lush bougainvillea. I got one photo before she jumped to the floor and got a second photo of her exposed derrière, her erect tail like a flag pole.

"Benny, in ten seconds check your phone for photos."

"Nothing, *boychik. Bupkis.*"

"Give it a half minute, Benny."

Twenty seconds passed.

"That's her ass. Why did you take a picture of her ass?"

"Check the next photo, for Christ's sake."

He acknowledged the second photo and that mollified him.

"She's a ravishing beauty, Benny. Everyone at the airport loved meeting her. My son thinks she's fantastic. Barry's so happy to have her with us."

"Jonathan, any time you see she's not well...you drop everything and get her to the vet. Send me the bill. I won't stick you with medical."

"Of course, Benny."

"Change her litter daily. Cats get sick from their excrement."

He hung up suddenly. I returned to the patio with my cold coffee. I lit a mini Brazilian cigar. I wanted to lounge in the sun and celebrate my new pet. In free association my mind conjured Paul Mazursky's

1970s road film, *Harry and Tonto*, starring Art Carney and an elderly cat named Tonto. Carney got an Oscar for portraying an old widower forced to vacate his Manhattan apartment. The pair go cross-country on a bus to Los Angeles. The cat dies in California. Harry finds a younger cat on the beach. Eureka!

Next time Benny calls, I'll ask him if he's an Art Carney fan. Carney and Jackie Gleason were pure genius in *The Honeymooners*. I'm more Carney than Gleason. I underact in the face of catastrophes. Yet catastrophes have special meaning for catastrophic Jews. And catastrophic Jews have an innate ability to anticipate disasters.

Death has come up into our windows, it has entered our palaces, to cut off the children from the streets and the young men from the squares –

Jeremiah 9:20.

Demonstrative religious speakers, authors, and proselytizers had suggested for months that the virus was God's wake-up call – the overture of humanity's mushrooming punishment. The 2020 pandemic could get exponentially worse. What should we learn from this terror, they asked us? Can contagion teach people how to conduct a meaningful life under threat of constant death? News shows posted the daily mortality rate and projected staggering future deaths by the end of 2020.

I didn't intuit that I would join the death toll but, statistically speaking, there would be friends and acquaintances who would succumb. All the while, Traci's ineluctable ghost seemed to shadow me. Behind each door and mirror. Spirits can be felt. She's in our house and in our yard, shimmering. Communicating with this unseen Traci was another matter.

Friends coached me to move to another address as a way of coping. How can I get on with life if I'm dwelling on her memory, they would say. I shrugged off the notion. I preferred living with all the physically anchored memories of Ariel, Barry and their mother. Even when Barry heads off to college, I will cherish the home. These last three years were a blur but a great amount of inner strength took hold for us.

The patio and garden signified a safe, contained serenity. I noticed this after returning from New York. Fretting about Ariel's whereabouts in October would simply throw more parental pain. She had vanished before for two or three days at a time. About a year ago end of summer, Ariel made it a five-day vanishing act. Even though we have a family iPhone plan, she won't allow me to track her. In my gut, something had gone badly for her. Her talent for resilience might be wanting. Adding to our family disrepair, Barry's rapport with Ariel had been dwindling since Traci's passing.

My phone pinged with a new message. It was Yunmei. She texted that her parents were in trouble and she asked if I could accept her phone call today. I texted back that she could call me anytime. Yunmei phoned a minute later.

"I'm sorry to bother you, Professor."

"That's fine. What's happening?"

"Things are very bad. My family wants me home now."

"Someone sick?"

"No. It's worse than that."

Her tone was strained and her breathing was heavy. Yunmei struggled with asthma.

"Government agents picked my parents up in a van on the way to work two days ago. They were held for questioning. They released my father after one day but held my mother for a second day."

"Why, Yunmei?"

"Security breach."

"You need to tell Columbia."

"That does nothing to help them."

"You never know. The Student Affairs office . . ."

"I went to Student Affairs on Zoom for another problem with my student visa, but they are idiots."

"Then go to Columbia's Office of International Students and Scholars."

"I did. They said they'll look into this."

"What are your parents telling you?"

"Very little. My father is very paranoid. His phone is being monitored."

"Then the government might be monitoring your phone." I said.

"One of my Chinese friends, Tianshi, re-posted my short video on jailing Hong Kong protestors and at the end of the video there is a half-minute coda on the reeducation camps."

"Your friend exposed you inadvertently, Yunmei?"

She was having trouble catching air.

"I know China monitors what we post without password protection. This adds to whatever they think my mother has done in the lab. She's very scared. She might lose her job."

"Have your friend take down the post."

"He did already. He thought I should try the Chinese Consulate."

"I don't think going to the Chinese Consulate will benefit your parents at this point."

"I want so badly to murder Xi Jinping."

And in her mind at this moment – so I imagined – the Chinese President was dead by a bullet to his head.

CHAPTER NINE

The instructions in my synagogue's PDF to congregational membership for observing the High Holy Days made it clear that in person assembly was not possible on the outside synagogue plaza. The synagogue leadership devised a plan to make online High Holy Days observances virtual and still maintain holy ritual. Synagogue participation would be as authentic as possible in each congregant's home. The congregation was instructed to schedule an appointment on one of the Sundays at the end of summer to pick up High Holy Day Home Haven packages. For those who didn't feel safe outside their homes, packages would be delivered by synagogue volunteers. One of the purposes of these physical appointments was to bestow on congregants the freedom to have a sacred, private moment at the synagogue while avoiding human density. Inside the prepared package was the Mahzor – the hefty High Holy Days prayer book – along with ritual and symbolic items. Congregants were encouraged to designate a space inside one's home that would serve as the area of prayer. Chairs used for this purpose, therefore, should not be used for other things until Yom Kippur concluded.

Congregants were encouraged to dress elegantly at home during online religious services, even if they were living alone. For any congregant or family grouping who had an ongoing "COVID bubble" with another congregant or family grouping, the synagogue encouraged High Holy Days collaborations outside in the yard.

For me, these prescriptions were both disappointing and also coincidental since the previous Yom Kippur I was reliant on YouTube observance during six days at an international conference at the Ingmar Bergman Foundation on the island of Fårö, Sweden. Fårö was a few hours by plane and bus from Stockholm, or eight hours by the less expensive ferry. In Sweden, the few synagogues were only in Stockholm and two municipalities far from Fårö. I selected two 2014 YouTube videos featuring Cantor Azi Schwartz of Park Avenue Synagogue celebrating Yom Kippur, and stayed in my Bergman Foundation cabin for the twenty four hour duration of Yom Kippur.

Rabbis everywhere would do their diligence classifying our pandemic as a world under threat. At the same time, rabbis would be calling to all to find their personal truth, test, and revelation. The Coronavirus, to Barry, was the insidious, shape shifting superior nemesis to Arnold Schwarzenegger in *Terminator 2/Judgment Day*. Like an all-powerful sci/fi threat from the near future, the Coronavirus in time could defeat us. Teens and young adults were becoming formidable superspreaders. Our nation had been inept to deal with this wisely and early, thinking we were protected by two great oceans. We had transgressed against native and acquired populations, enslaved and incarcerated people, harmed the animal kingdom. We had ruined the air, water and land we now occupy. We harmed ourselves. We had violated the essential compact found in Martin Buber's *I and Thou*. The virus was not simply an accident in an Asian wet market.

Sunday morning Barry met me in the kitchen brewing coffee. He was in pajama bottoms and shirtless. He had aged in the last six months. His face had an etched seriousness. Barry said that I looked thinner. He said that high school was getting ridiculous with hybrid in-person and online structure cooked up last month. The in-person component was little more than office hours and small group tutorials. Despite his prescription of Adderall, he found the curriculum and presentation too boring this semester, on the heels of a lackluster online spring semester. I argued that this was his last transcript for college applications and he had to power through the semester. Barry said that some friends were going to take the year off gambling that the vaccine won't be widely in play for college freshman year. He brought up Ariel, expressing his own prediction.

"She's not coming back, Dad."

"What do you mean?"

"Like she's done with us."

"Did she tell you that?"

"No. But you knew how angry she gets."

"She'll need money."

"Yeah. She'll always need money."

"Did you just talk to each other?"

"She broke up with her boyfriend."

"This week?"

"I think so."

"I can't stand her boyfriend."

"Yeah, he's a dick." Barry stated in monotone.

"Why the hell did she ever pick him?"

"Beach party bonfire."

"How is it that I never met him?"

"She knew you'd pick a fight once you saw him."

"Really?"

"Nick's got that look. From his hair to his boots. He went to Juvenile Detention Center for a couple of months."

"Oh?"

"Stealing a car. His family's Audi. His folks called the cops. "

This news threw me. Barry's attention went to his iPad as he was viewing a tutorial on installing more RAM into a desktop.

"Is she staying with a Nick or a girlfriend this week?"

"She doesn't have any real girlfriends." Barry's voice had drifted.

"Why is that?"

"She thinks all the girls are hitting on him."

Barry smiled tightly showing a chord of pain or harsh judgment.

"That's that." I said.

"Nick moves like a desert iguana. His skin has scales."

"Drugs?"

Barry shook his head. I wasn't supposed to know either.

"Will you join me tonight for Yom Kippur?"

"It's not working for me, Dad."

"You went the last few years."

"That was to help you get through Mom."

"Thank you."

He had sympathy for me and he was being honest. I let the matter drop but craved a little more conversation.

"Do you have a girlfriend?" I asked.

"No."

He was annoyed that I asked this, more annoyed than asking about Yom Kippur.

"Sorry for asking."

"I wouldn't tell you if I did." he replied.

"You don't have to tell me anything."

"Good, Dad."

"You've an active internet life. I'm clueless about your world."

"Clueless is almost right."

"What are you really thinking, Barry?"

"I can't stand COVID life. I hate online school and masks. And I worry about you."

"Really?"

"Why don't you date? It's overdue, Dad. You're spending too much time alone. You're becoming a freak."

"A freak?"

"Not literally. But yeah, a freak. Mom would have dated, if you had cancer."

"You think so?"

Barry went back into his room after pouring orange juice into the tallest glass in the kitchen. I took sanctuary in the patio. Parenting makes us as stupid as a rock, more so if you are left alone in the final years before the age of eighteen. Barry's college years would be manageable. I sensed that in my heart and that was my hope. Since Traci's passing, I wondered how many years before retiring. College was a buffer to my internal family issues and to the growing fixation on mortality. Still, Zoom lectures and seminars had destroyed the joys of teaching and the department was drifting to a woke chokehold. Artistic freedom of expression was no longer a prevailing virtue. Virtue signalling was trending like wildfire. There was news last June from our department that a student committee was formed to review syllabi of all classes in support of correcting our embarrassing deficit of diversity and anti-racism content. The student committee had a zealous faculty advisor. Horowitz and an ad hoc tiger team had updated radically the department bylaws which were voted on electronically during the summer. Questions will arise down the road about how to protect academic freedom under assertive didactic prescriptions, unsubtle arm twisting, and curricula ultimatums. Even though I taught the films of Spike Lee every other year, my bandwidth appeared heavily European and not proactive in the wake of George Floyd's murder. Acaemic retirement before hitting the age of seventy had been the norm. Retirement at my campus, once chosen, cannot be undone. A retirement party in this cultural climate from my department would not be any more glorious than a eulogy in front of an open coffin.

As Sunday unfolded, I spent time with the cat and cleaned the litter. I was getting better at this chore and used the N95 to avoid the odor. I felt fatigue from the New York travel and serious concern about Yunmei's situation. I made a note to myself to contact Student Affairs and our International House on my campus to see what protections could be afforded to an alum. Most colleges would invariably pass the buck to Columbia, but I was keen to know what few protections exist against the Chinese government and their international students. It would be ludicrous if I went to the Chinese Consulate in Los Angeles on her behalf and I might risk making matters worse for her. Yunmei held my mind this week more than Ariel, making me doubt my priorities as a father.

CHAPTER TEN

There were more emails with attachments from Yunmei sent Monday to my Gmail. One letter had photos of her parents in formal wedding poses and in their medical labs. The most curious photo was a family vacation at a lake. Yunmei was a young adolescent in that shot, her arm around her father. Her mother, wearing sunglasses and a wide brim hat, was standing alone, her mouth open – an expression of surprise or annoyance? Her father wore a yellow polo shirt and his sunglasses were atop his head. He was bald with distinguished grey around the temples. Yunmei's smile matched her father's. The family looked happy and spontaneous. Yunmei described the photo as an occasion when the family enjoyed ordinary life. There was also a small, white dog, off to the side and seated, making a celebratory statement about summer in pastoral China.

I didn't think it was improper to check my email during Yom Kippur, although I set my phone on mute. Routine business was to be shunned on this most holy day. Per the synagogue's recommendation, I did place two extra chairs inside my home office. I knew that Barry wouldn't be sitting with me and, therefore, the spare chair for symbolism. Traci hadn't converted to Judaism so the chair wasn't for her. I accepted the second seat as a Jewish statement of welcoming the metaphorical stranger at the door.

Last year at this time, watching from Sweden Yom Kippur services on YouTube felt as connective as watching my synagogue's rabbi and cantor on live feed. Cyberspace observance adumbrated futuristic self-quarantine venues. Last night I heard Kol Nidre beamed from my house of worship three miles away. It was moving, yet distancing. Kol Nidre was the capstone of the High Holy Days. Singing Kol Nidre within earshot of his dying father had been the climax of Al Jolson's landmark *The Jazz Singer*. Yom Kippur concluded the Ten Days of Awe. The metaphoric Book of Life, opened at Rosh Hashanah, served the demarcation of the Jewish New Year. Reflection and atonement overrode everything. The Book of Life recorded the names forever of all people considered good and righteous. To be blotted out of this Book assigned death and spiritual obliteration. It was with this allusion to the Book of Life that the holy remnant was spoken of as being written unto life in Jerusalem. All, who shall be found, entered into the Book of Life. Would that state encompass eternal bliss? Would we reunite with loved ones gone? I looked at the empty chair next to mine.

Cassandra had accepted the office space as her terrain. She had sneezed earlier today and yesterday. I didn't know cats can sneeze. She favored my upholstered office chair. I took photos of her today and texted them to Benny with a short message in Hebrew: *G'mar Hatima Tova* – May you be sealed in the Book of Life.

To the best of my knowledge, Benny had identified as Jewish and was proud of his heritage as he donated millions of dollars to United Jewish Appeal over thirty years. If I had to bet, Benny Edelmann had not set foot inside a synagogue since Jewish pitcher Sandy Koufax retired from baseball in 1966.

In the morning Yom Kippur service, my thoughts were pinned to Ariel's future. I was obsessing about her. She was in my prayers. Pulling away from her, I was yearning to be back with Traci in her last year with us. My thoughts also sailed around the Jeunet/Gilliam book. The tome was important to me but something in the final chapter inhibited a proper finish. My Michigan Press editor implored me to assume a critical preference whereby I would be catapulting one director over the other. I had published with this press before and I trusted their editorial role. I also missed the early deadline and Michigan knew I was quite reliable on timetables.

Film was becoming too artificial for me this year. This season of our discontent I was detached and unmoved from the visual dexterity of Jean-Pierre Jeunet and Terry Gilliam. These filmmakers represented aesthetic values of a faraway universe as we struggle with a contagion.

The other thought that bombarded me during Yom Kippur service was my confusion over my parents' lack of committed Jewish faith. They had demanded that I embrace Hebrew school and religious holidays, all the while demonstrating their own incurious ties to Judaism. To a pre-teen this appeared like hypocracy. My grandparents were more observant to Jewish ritual. I rediscovered Judaism after my father's death by saying *kaddish* for eleven months during graduate school. Faith lessened the darkness after his passing. During my passages of life, I had weaved in and out of faith. My children had no feeling for this Judaism after the age of thirteen. Judaism seemed to be skipping every other generation within my family tree.

I made a pasta for Barry and me, breaking my fast around seven o'clock. He wolfed down his plate. Barry told me that he had watched *The Lighthouse,* which he gave four stars for its intense insanity between two men – one young, one old – trapped by harsh physical nature, madness and something otherworldly. This apparently was director Robert Eggers' take on the Edgar Allan Poe tale with the similar title. *The Lighthouse* was not filmed in color, according to Barry, and the design lent itself to the palette of shadow. In my son's one minute review, Willem Dafoe played the lighthouse keeper as if he literally ingested a demonic brew of turpentine and honey as outlined in the screenplay.

It was fortunate that we had a subject to discuss at the table and that Barry was beginning to sound like a professor. Dinner was interrupted by an incoming call on Barry's cell. He left for his room. I cleared the plates. Ten minutes later Celeste rang me.

"How was your fast?" she asked.

"Fine, Celeste."

"I fast all the time. Fasting stops my migraines."

"Aren't you taking medication for them?"

She cleared her throat.

"No medication. No acupuncture. Nothing works but cleansing fasts. I'm glad you're free to talk now."

"It's been a quiet day. Conversation would be good."

"Our last talk was tough. And I'm sorry how I said things."

I didn't know what to say in response.

"My marriage isn't good. You knew that a long time ago."

"Yes."

"You told me to avoid marrying Tony."

"Yes."

"You're aware of a lot of stuff. More than my close friends here. Seeing you in New York excited me. You're looking vulnerable. Please don't be pissed about things that are in our past."

"I'm not pissed, Celeste."

"Good. I don't believe things are predestined. But look at where we both are this year."

"We both have broken hearts."

I had no energy for the direction of this conversation. I didn't sense Celeste was manipulating emotional logic. She told me two incidents with her second husband which had underscored her judgments. I did want to know the details even if hearing them compromised things. Celeste found in the laundry a business card for an escort service, which Tony had protested vehemently. It was a card circulated among some men at the office, according to Tony. He called it a bad joke. Even if Celeste and Tony were attempting an open marriage, prostitution was completely out of bounds in her view. The second incident was more repulsive. Celeste went through Tony's browser history in his bedroom laptop and found that he was visiting lurid sites featuring underage teens. She had confronted him while visiting Tony's mother in New Rochelle and his mother threw an empty vase at Celeste, missing Celeste but destroying her dining room hutch. Celeste went back to their Manhattan apartment. Her husband stayed in New Rochelle.

"He's a sick man."

"Yes."

"I'm a mess, Jonathan."

"You're not."

"We tried counselling for a year. What a travesty that was."

"Maybe a separation?"

"Separation isn't a brave step, Jonathan. I'll call an attorney this week." She then paused for long moment. "I was thinking about your daughter this weekend."

"Thanks."

"Maybe I could talk to her?"

"It wouldn't help."

"I could pretend to be as good as an aunt."

"Celeste."

"Nothing wrong with a phone call. I'll say that I'll be in L.A. mid-October and thought I could swing down to San Diego."

"The timing is not great."

"Why?" she said softly.

"Too close to Halloween."

"We'll just have dinner at your favorite restaurant, Jonathan."

"What prompted you to talk about an abortion?"

"I don't know. I'm sorry."

She led herself into an inner monologue about wanting another child. Having only a daughter, she declared, felt incomplete. Celeste had imagined that the abortion blocked the birth of a son. She had owned the responsibility of the decision made long ago but that had not mitigated the yearning. Celeste admonished her life's choices and what she had perceived as a dangerous need for love from others. She was convincing over the phone. I found myself feeding on her confessions. I agreed that an outdoor dinner in San Diego next month would be very good for both of us.

"I'll only drive down from L.A. if you really want to see me."

"I want to see you, Celeste."

"When does Barry go to college?"

"Next fall."

"Will he leave California?"

"I doubt it. One of the state's public campuses."

"That's good for both of you."

"Yes."

"You know, Traci talked to me about how she grabbed you from me."

"Really?"

"How many years of mourning for her do you need?"

She ended the call.

I fed the cat and changed the cat's water dish. I turned on the television. Cable news went on about the death toll. This prodded me to open the word document on the film book. I dove into the final chapter and forced the typist inside to find words. I flipped a coin that was on my desk. Heads, I would argue that Jeunet was the superior visionary. Tails, Gilliam. The dime spun in the air, bounced off the desk, and landed at my feet. It was heads.

CHAPTER ELEVEN

Tuesday morning I got a text from Jason Horowitz. He asked if he could call late morning and said it was important. I texted back yes. Horowitz qualified in his response that it would be better to hold the conversation on Zoom. That meant brushing one's hair. I didn't know if the chair was pursuing me for missing yesterday's faculty meeting or if this was about accepting a convoluted service assignment above my normal workload. Of course, there was Gerhardt's predicament with Brenda Whitaker which might supercede everything today. I went with the Zoom request assuming the video camera being turned on was *de rigueur*. I also got a text from Benny who exclaimed his joy after seeing more photos of his cat. Benny said he was having some night chills and thought it was the result of getting the shingles shot from his assisted living Jamaican nurse Hanna who sang Bob Marley to him.

I was reading the Times on my iPad when the Zoom alert was triggered. I turned on my camera and saw Horowitz wearing a polka dot necktie at home. His thinning hair was combed by a blind barber.

"Hey…good morning, Jonathan."

"Good morning, Jason."

"Thanks for taking the call. I know this is the weekend. How was your time in New York?"

"All good. Nice to go east for a week."

"So I know you missed the faculty meeting but you should read the minutes in the Google drive. We are moving forward in extending graduate matriculation half a year. That's the mood most of us have embraced. This will cost the department but we anticipate that subsequent graduate cohorts coming in will be less in number. The students were polled and hoped we could move in this direction. If you haven't voted yet on the measure, you can get to the electronic ballot by 6pm today."

"Okay."

"Okay." Horowitz parroted politely.

Zoom tries to telegraph within interpersonal sessions that eye contact is lifelike and functioning. Horowitz was scoping me out about his agenda. He didn't strike a genuine note even when he smiled broadly.

"You and I know Oscar a long time. He's a closer friend to you. We've trouble again, embarrassing to the department. I'm certain that he called you."

"He did."

"Good."

"Is it that bad, Jason?"

"It is."

"What happens now?"

"We are almost finished with our ad hoc review before turning this over to the central office. Oscar states that you witnessed Brenda Whitaker invite him to her apartment for dinner."

"No."

"No, you didn't witness this or no, you don't want to make a statement?"

"Are you recording this conversation, Jason?"

"You would see the Zoom record icon if I were recording."

"I'm an idiot about Zoom."

"Well, you're no Luddite."

"I didn't witness Brenda saying anything like that to Oscar. She's thoroughly professional and reserved. I never saw anything inappropriate from either party."

"Did you see her flirt with him? Or his flirting with her?"

"No."

"Did she ever flirt with you?"

"No. Never. I don't have much dealing with Brenda."

"But she was in one of your seminars?"

"Yes, she was in one seminar about a year ago."

"Do you find her attractive?"

"Why are you asking me that, Jason?"

"I wasn't casting aspersions."

I wanted to end the Zoom session with a simple Luddite click.

"Jason, these faculty ad hoc reviews are redundant. They have little bearing if the campus office to prevent sexual harassment intercedes."

"Why probe this from your office, Jason?"

"We use the ad hoc reviews smartly. Several instances never make it to the central office. But off the record, Brenda has several witnesses validating her grievance to my office."

"Why isn't she going directly to the campus office, Jason?"

"I don't know. The vice chair and I gave her the option. She might fear retaliation and career damage if the central office investigates."

"Is there anything else or are we done?" I asked.

"Do you think Oscar can't control himself? Is he on medication?"

"What I think or what I know isn't relevant to Brenda's complaint."

"Everything is relevant, Jonathan. Withholding is no virtue."

Horowitz and I lapsed into an awkward silence as we looked at our computer screens. He had a virtual backdrop of the Golden Gate Bridge. I just sat in front of my bookshelf. The call was essentially over and I could glean that Oscar Gerhardt was months away from losing his job. He had to have been desperate to fabricate things which involved me.

I was tired of focusing on Gerhardt's vices. The noise in my head centered around Yunmei's crisis. Horowitz should assume some responsibility for our alumni from China who have political issues.

"Jason, can I switch the topic?"

"We're not done with Oscar."

"I thought we were."

"Did you cover for him regarding the postdoc incident?"

"No, I didn't. I'm not built that way."

"I really don't know how you're built, Jonathan."

"I have ethics, Jason." I took a long breath. "We've a Chinese alum at Columbia in her first year who seems to be in serious trouble with the Chinese authorities. She's a lit major, graduated a year ago, an only child."

"What's the trouble?"

"Video postings on blogs and social media very critical of the government. Her parents were detained for questioning. Her parents are doctors and one also got into trouble recently."

Horowitz formed a quizzical, moronic expression between his brow and upper chin.

"What is her name?"

"Yunmei Yang. I believe that her parents are prominent research physicians in Beijing."

"Why are you in communication with her?"

"She's a gifted film student. Came to office hours weekly. I wrote her recommendation letter."

"Let Columbia handle it. Columbia has a presence in China and more leverage with Beijing than our campus."

"I realize. It just seemed stronger to work with Columbia to help her family."

"Go ahead and contact our Dean, Jonathan. I'll back you up."

"Thank you."

"And I'll keep your statements about Gerhardt confidential. He won't know the specifics if he asks me."

"Good."

The platform of Zoom with campus calls like this seemed sinister and Orwellian. There's something backchannel about Zoom – hiding a pugnacious grand inquisitor with legal pad to review each video. Jason was recording the Zoom call. Had this exchange with Jason Horowitz happened over the phone, it would be still be disagreeable but not creepy. Horowitz projected false compassion. He functioned as if following a script approved by a committee on academic governance and conflict resolution. He didn't care if his performance as chair in the Gerhardt issue was humane or bureaucratic. He simply had to hit all the check boxes. The call was perfunctory. Horowitz would not lose sleep over Gerhardt's dismissal. To Horowitz, purging the department of Gerhardt, the chronic predator of younger women, would be heroic. And yes, younger faculty were coveting Gerhardt's large corner office with a window over the recreational field and ocean.

"Jonathan, I wish you can appreciate my position. Chairing a large department is a pain in the ass. A good chair caters to every professor, staffer, student, and alum all the while mollifying upper administration. A superb chair is no better than a suave hotel concierge who quotes Proust and Baudelaire effortlessly."

I had to laugh. Horowitz went on like a logorrheic machine.

"Balancing the budget during COVID is horrid. We're facing 10% permanent cuts and a hiring freeze until 2025. We are laying off staff. If we lose Oscar Gerhardt, we cannot hire his successor. His conduct costs us double. To make matters worse, we have early retirements coming. You're not thinking of retiring?"

"No, not for another five years."

"Good. How do you stay fit? Tennis?"

"No tennis."

"And you're productive. Still publishing at your age."

"Jason, are we done?"

"With the aftermath of the George Floyd murder, we can't teach old syllabi. The nation exalted him into our new Jesus. Floyd shook the world. We have to recruit minority students with every tool we possess. Our grad students are up in arms. Really, a white straight cis-male should not be the chair."

"Why not step down, Jason?"

"I signed for a three-year term."

"Get a doctor's note about stress. Most doctors will write one on request."

"Very funny."

"I'm serious."

"I'm sorry your former student is in the crosshairs of the Chinese government. She'll end up losing her student visa. China won't permit dissent. Her parents might disown her to survive. In twenty years China will be the only global superpower. We're like Great Britain at the end of World War I."

I said nothing but my face looked grim on Zoom. Certainly, Horowitz was making some effort to be human. I had to give him the benefit of the doubt. He was always the consummate asshole who reminded faculty once a year that he was an Eagle Scout. He stopped publishing long work after 9/11 and had pivoted to editing anthologies as a way to tread water. Horowitz pressed the Zoom kill button which ended our meeting.

It seemed necessary to tell Oscar that he had no more lifelines. Knowing him well, it would be better to meet for a beer. Oscar would berate me much more in person for failing him but I would feel better facing that assault. I decided to text Oscar about the decisions coming from Horowitz. Oscar needed a good lawyer to litigate this mess if he was determined to fight for his job. Best case scenario, Oscar Gerhardt would get a lump sum to leave the university and campus communications will keep this scandal from media outlets. Oscar had a daughter Penelope at a Midwest college who resembled him from chin to brow. He had sizable overhead and a mortgage to consider. I don't see him living out of a camper-van on a Costco parking lot but I have seen some talented people entering that zone.

Checking email, I received a formal note from New Montefiore Cemetery stating in concise terms that management had no idea how my mother's grave was damaged. New Montefiore downplayed the incident. It was a natural phenomenon cemeteries had seen before. Hedgehogs and moles have destroyed some graves over the years. New Montefiore management apologized. Perhaps – their letter articulated – this was caused by a sinkhole at night. Management stated that Long Island had experienced sporadic sinkholes. Jan 13, 2013, a car was swallowed whole by a Smithtown sinkhole. October 30, 2012, after Hurricane Sandy, Woodmere suffered a destructive sinkhole. In Oceanside, on October 30, 2011, an eighty-year-old man was sucked into a lawn pit while getting the morning paper. New Montefiore assured me that landscaping would prioritize my mother's grave. There was no mention that vandalism ever occurred at their cemetery.

CHAPTER TWELVE

After serving Barry dinner from our charcoal barbeque, I taught my second evening class of fall term on Zoom. The film noir course touched favorites from the 1940s–1960s and I centered on Alfred Hitchcock's work. Usually I liked to indulge in the agile, dry ironic pictures Hitchcock applied to his peak years 1954–1964, a period of Hollywood filmmaking which enticed my tastes. I fell in love with movies as a boy and Hitchcock hooked me early. He was thoroughly deft delineating good and evil, innocence and deception. Morally upstanding characters in Hitchcock films had to burn through their burden of American simpleness and gullibility in order to survive. *Rear Window* played with a clever concept of voyeurism starring a very vulnerable James Stewart. Recuperating from a leg injury, Stewart's character – a photographer with a broken leg – is confined to a wheelchair in his Manhattan apartment. His window fronts a courtyard and many apartments. During a heat wave, he spies his neighbors – their windows open – and pieces together circumstances leading him to suspect a murder committed by the dark hulking character played by Raymond Burr. Hitchcock was wise choosing Burr, who was terrifying absent of dialogue. Two years after *Rear Window*, Burr had launched his television career as the flawless criminal defense attorney in *Perry Mason* based on the novels by Erle Stanley Gardner. Burr's acting range was thrilling, even if Perry Mason became his eternal brand. I showed clips from Hitchcock's other works, even a snippet of *Perry Mason*, and assigned *Rear Window* from the library digital reserve. Voyeurism was a running theme in Hitchcock's canon and voyeurism became a theme for David Lynch and Lynch's generation.

There was a game I played at dinner parties whereby I would insert persons known to the party into the James Stewart role. Dinner friends would try to imagine these folks ward off Raymond Burr in the final, roller coaster segment of *Rear Window*. Hitchcock's killer raced to knock off the apartment building voyeur immobilized by a wheel chair. Benny Edelmann would most likely use his broomstick to fight off Raymond Burr. Jason Horowitz would assemble an ad hoc committee. Celeste would take him out with her mace spray on her key chain. Once when I was very high, I had cast myself in the Stewart role playing a harmonica and singing a Neil Young song as my absolute defense.

Stepping back to my office I checked on the cat and to force myself into the Michigan Press book. Cassandra was asleep in her favorite new chair. Cassandra felt like invaluable company. Her face and torso projected serenity. I began typing pithy paragraphs which advanced the book in a proper direction. No notes were used. The theoretical logic was self-evident based on the previous chapters. I was composing a conclusion and a narrative which argued that these two iconoclastic film directors weren't in a competition but they seemed to influence one another with their respective aesthetics and mischief. Gilliam preceded Jeunet chronologically and championed Jeunet early on but at some point in time these artists had to have been quite conscious of one another. Both filmmakers took aim at adolescence and how their adult heroes were holding on to the purity of their innocence. Jeunet had praised Gilliam on several occasions, but the two men had met only twice. They gave an interview together for *Studio* magazine. Gilliam generated a line on the poster of Jeunet's second film, *The City of Lost Children*, to assist the release of the film. Both artists had been very enamored of the wild capacity of film animation and non-realistic escapism.

As I was finishing my manuscript, Yunmei texted a long, disturbing message. Her family crisis grew worse. She didn't want to fly to Beijing, despite dire requests from her parents. She knew her parents were set to capitulate. Her mother would go to prison if there were no cooperation with China and the family house would be seized. Yunmei said she was left with two thousand dollars in her New York bank account. Once that was gone, she would be in trouble. She decided to break with her family and retaliate against China's authority.

I also received a longer email from her. Yunmei admitted to her paranoia and stopped taking medication to offset her anxiety. She thought of several outlandish plots. She could self-immolate like a Tibetan monk in front of the Chinese consulate at 520 12th Avenue. She could construct rice pressure cooker bombs under consulate cars parked along the avenue. Yunmei studied websites hosting tutorial videos on making bombs. Yunmei had lost her mind in short of a few days. It wasn't clear to me how quickly she would be resolute with her next action, but I was horrified about her mental health and the danger she might orchestrate. I tried to phone. I composed a few clumsy thoughts and texted them.

Yunmei, please don't act on your emotions this week.
You could help your parents by flying home.
They really need your help. Fly home.
If you fear travel, you should stay.
Don't worry about money.
Get back on medication.
Contact campus counseling services.
Don't commit to any violent action.
Let me help. Let me contact Columbia.
I can send you cash. Call me anytime.
Don't post anything online.
Please stay safe.

I sent the same message in an email. I was thoroughly unnerved by this. Yunmei wasn't the person to make idle threats. She once brought up during office hours reports of a dozen self-immolations in China's Sichuan, Qinghai and Gansu Province around 2013. Most of the victims were young Buddhist monks and their family members.

I couldn't intuit whether Yunmei was experiencing extreme fragility or was empowered by the furies. She was the most isolated and introverted college student I have ever met. Would she return my phone call? What else was there to do?

My eyes glanced at Cassandra who was watching me. I imagined Benny's old gritty voice and how he might comment on my concern for a Chinese student. Benny had street smarts which was something I lacked. The tough, leather jacket Jews of lower Manhattan circa 1950s would not suffer fools gladly. I guessed that Benny would tell me to send the girl ten thousand dollars and be done with her. He would say that she wasn't worth the bother.

Benny Edelmann resembled literary critic Irving Howe – the two men had a very similar pout, broad tortoiseshell eyeglasses, and grey driver cap. Howe, once a strident socialist and probably fifteen years older than Benny, was hounded by a Stanford radical and he shot the student with, "You know what you're going to be in ten years? A goddamn dentist."

Benny was not short of wisdom, but he only asked of his efficient mind to commit necessary actions. Theory for theory's sake was bullshit to Benny. Life's question was how much cash remained on the table and who was chicken shit. Benny's career was vested in sniffing out human weakness. He had thought that libraries only attracted dust mites and book lice. There was one dinner I shared with my father and Benny where Benny surprised us by reciting Robert Frost:

> *Two roads diverged in a yellow wood,*
> *And sorry I could not travel both*
> *And be one traveler, long I stood*
> *And looked down one as far as I could*
> *To where it bent in the undergrowth;*

If there was a way to dispatch Benny to Beijing for thirty-six hours, Yunmei's crisis would vanish. There were canny foreign affairs brokers like Henry Kissinger and Madeleine Albright – biological Jews – who cut through conventional straitjackets. But why did God invent Benny Edelmann for the shadier side of American capitalism?

In my bones I knew I had to do something decisive and immediate for Yunmei.

The days ahead had challenged my priorities. Foremost was to contact a San Diego police friend if Ariel extended her disappearance into a second week. The least pressing task was to find a grad student to adopt the cat. Gerhardt was a mounting problem. Yunmei's precarious status was of utmost concern. Yunmei might very well harm herself.

My phone rang after 10pm. I thought this was Ariel coming back into orbit, but it was a call with a New York City area code which I couldn't recognize. I took the call.

"Jonathan?"

The voice was gruff. It was Benny.

"Past 1am in New York, Benny. Kind of late?"

"Just can't sleep tonight. Ate something spicy. I'm a dumb fuck."

"How's your cough?"

"All better. Nyquil and scotch."

"I worried that you might have picked up the virus."

"Yeah, me too. Can't kiss anybody anymore."

"Benny, I don't recognize this phone number."

"I got two cell phones. The other one is charging. Listen, I want to tell you something."

"What Benny?"

"Your old man was a strong sonofabitch."

"I know."

"You don't know. He put on a white lace show for you."

"What do you mean?"

"Your father wasn't a gangster, but he had balls. Never took shit from anyone. Maybe in his late teens he had a few rackets. He made jokes about some dark shit in the garment district. He was good getting idiots out of debt and collecting cash. He had muscle."

"Benny, why are you telling me this and at this hour?"

"I had this impulse, Jonathan. You need to know."

"That's not my father."

"Your mother never knew."

"My father was never a racketeer."

"No, he wasn't. That's a true statement. But let me tell you a story about when your dad came by my house in Queens. My boy Maxie was playing ball on the stoop and he hit the window of a trucker. The trucker was pissed and took his rubber ball. Maxie's about three years older than you. Your father often came by to visit us to break up his work day. He was a salesman on calls. Well, he saw Maxie crying like a baby. He took Maxie by the hand and asked to point out the moron. My wife followed them to the stoop. Outside the trucker was still parked, his engine idling. Your father knocked on the glass and the trucker rolled down the window. He said, "Did you take my nephew's rubber ball?"

Benny paused for effect.

"Yeah, I took the kid's ball."

"Your father punched him out and the trucker screamed loud enough to wake the dead in Forest Lawn. Maxie got the ball back."

"That's quite a story, Benny."

"Your old man was like an uncle to Maxie."

"Why are you telling me this?"

"I miss your father."

Silence.

"Thanks for the call. I need to go to bed."

"Not yet, Jonathan."

"Benny..."

"Five more minutes. I'm such a sucker for nostalgia."

"So was my old man, Benny."

"You're the link. That's who you are. Did you know that the Jewish character Hyman Roth in *The Godfather* movies played by Lee Strasberg was based on the gangster Meyer Lansky? Did you know that after the movie opened, Lansky phoned Strasberg and congratulated him on great acting?"

"Never knew that."

"It's true, boychik. Lansky told Strasberg, 'but you could've made me more sympathetic.'"

"That's funny, Benny."

"I met Strasberg at the Plaza Hotel eight years before Trump bought the hotel. Strasberg died two years later – 1982. Listen Jonathan. Your father Myron did something once for me that I'll never forget. Very brave. This is why I fronted him cash to start his business."

"I don't want to know."

There was no stopping Benny. He had to unload his bucket of shit.

"I'll make this short. I had some serious trouble in the Bronx. And I had to blame someone close to me so I could get home with my head on my neck. I got Myron involved and he had nothing to do with my fucking problem. Do you know what I'm trying to say?"

I made a muffled sound to respond.

"He took a beating that week. It was a bad bruising. They broke his nose and collar bone. I told your father that I would make it up to him. This goes beyond the money that launched his auto dealership. So what I'm trying to say is that your name is in my will. Maxie doesn't know."

"What?" I muttered stupified.

"Did you hear what I just said?"

"No."

"You're named in my will. I owe Myron."

"No, Benny. I don't want anything from you."

"This has nothing whatsoever to do with Cassandra."

Benny abruptly hung up.

CHAPTER THIRTEEN

Wednesday morning I brewed coffee before sunrise. There must have been a brief power outage since the kitchen clock lost time. No need to drive Barry to school since the county had determined online teaching was required for K-12 grades through fall semester. State and county were adhering to the spiking data charts. Many area private schools with small populations had waivers allowing in person instruction. Barry had to be awake by first period on Zoom, 8:30am, but he didn't have to change out of his pajamas. He loved this freedom. He loved PJs.

I made a pot of coffee, bit an apple, and added a slice of dry toast to a yogurt breakfast. There was a hummingbird outside the kitchen window. Cassandra made her first appearance inside our kitchen. The New York Times headlines indicated that we were inching towards a civil war on race. The Black Lives Matter movement broke historic records on participation and took the powerful shape of a lasting movement. Will Democrats get hurt irrevocably in the upcoming election if they're branded as the party advocating disbanding the police?

The doorbell rang. I guessed this was San Diego Gas and Electric about another brown out due to the wildfires, but it was Gerhardt standing outside. I opened the door halfway worried the cat was loose and not confined to the office. Oscar Gerhardt appeared disheveled, and looking wholly out of character.

"Morning, Jonathan."

"Good morning."

"Here's your campus mail. I went by the building last night."

"Oscar, what's going on?"

"I didn't want to phone."

"You look awful."

"Can I come in?"

I took the mail and let him inside with a wave of one hand. Oscar, in face mask, had on a necktie.

"I know you talked to Horowitz." he said.

"He asked me about you and Brenda."

"I thought we would get our stories straight, Jonathan, before Horowitz called."

I led him into the patio which was farthest from Barry's room.

"Do you want coffee?"

"No."

"I told Horowitz what was true. But nothing incriminating."

"Everything can be incriminating with Horowitz as chair."

"This isn't about Jason Horowitz, Oscar."

"Horowitz's a scumbag."

"So?"

"I thought you would be a better friend. I came to your aid when the department faulted you for showing Jodorowsky's *El Topo* in class."

"I can't lie to give you cover."

"You wouldn't be lying. You just have to say that Brenda created an opening."

"That would be fiction."

"She slept with a visiting professor from the history department."

"Keep your voice down, Oscar. My son's home."

This was getting uncomfortable with Gerhardt's face reddening.

"She fucked Bloomberg."

"Who's Bloomberg?"

"The visiting professor. He's in his thirties. Yes, I have it from a good source."

"So what? That doesn't help your case."

"You don't believe a word I say."

Gerhardt paced the patio. He was scaring the sparrows. He slipped the mask down to his chin. It looked like he nicked himself shaving this morning. I sat down hoping that he would settle into a functional calm. He lowered his voice. From his face I could discern Gerhardt's sense of failure. This was too much intimacy with a work friend. He was telegraphing a new depth of desperation. All the years we have known each other, here was the moment Gerhardt displayed his meaningless world. He may have led a charmed life with amazing career breaks, published rave reviews, and the proverbial hall pass when trapped by his impulsive behavior. A talented therapist could coax him into a survival plan teaching adjunct at a community college, editing at an academic press, perhaps trying physical work at a state park to make a full break from literature. But Gerhardt was too proud to follow any therapist's suggestion.

"Maybe, Oscar," I started to say, "you make an appointment tomorrow with the campus office of prevention of harassment and discrimination to get ahead of this case?"

"And say what?"

"That you just began therapy on impulse control. You didn't touch Brenda?"

"I won't go back to therapy."

"That's the 'old you'. The 'new you' will go once a week for a couple of years."

"It won't be enough. They already have a file on me."

"Try it, Oscar. It might work."

"Brenda will say I touched her."

"Did you?"

"I might have kissed her on the cheek at an evening poetry reception."

"That's not good. What else, Oscar?"

"Nothing more. Talk to Brenda and plead with her that I've one child with special needs in college."

"Why would she change her story for me?"

"You're sympathetic." said Gerhardt.

"It would be compromising herself, and you put me at risk if she reports me exerting influence."

"She respects you. I know that much."

"Start therapy this week."

"You're a selfish sonofabitch."

"I'm an old friend who cares."

"You don't care. Stop bullshitting me, Klein."

Gerhardt raced out of the patio. I heard his car take off. This was getting worse by the hour. He achieved one thing this morning, injecting a dollop of guilt into my head. He only referenced me by my surname when we're with colleagues at a party or shouting in the parking lot. Had I known Brenda Whitaker better, I might have risked a conversation without lobbying. There was nothing to do at this point. Horowitz would move forward and consequences would hit Oscar Gerhardt quickly.

I met my son in the kitchen.

"Who was that?"

"A faculty friend." I replied. "You know him. Oscar Gerhardt."

"Didn't sound like fun, Dad."

"A lot of faculty are grappling with burnout."

Barry nodded. I made him breakfast. I thought about telling Barry the ugly absurdity of last night's call from Benny, conveying an anecdote about his grandfather that might be utterly delusional. Barry never met his grandfather from either side of his family tree. That came from parenting late. I was finding solace in recent exchanges with my son. He was making an effort validating difficult things that were happening in our lives and his commiseration demonstrated the powers of young manhood. I decided that nothing about Benny's call was worth relating to my son.

"I finished my new film book for Michigan Press."

"Cool." he said.

"Want to read it?"

"No."

"Okay." I said.

There was a pause. He sensed the silence too. So he changed the trail we were on.

"What do you think of the George Floyd and Breonna Taylor's murders?"

"Appalling. Heartbreaking." I said.

"America is a racist nation." said Barry.

"Yeah. Two societies that collide. Obama was a great president. We strive in vain to build a free and safe world. Cops keep doing this."

"Cops have to be retrained." he said.

"Definitely. And screened better at time of hire."

The kitchen was our town hall. Barry affected an Irish accent for his zinger.

"Excuse me language, Dad, but fuck Trump."

"I'm with you, Barry."

"He's screwed everybody not inside his camp."

"He lost the popular vote by nearly three million."

"And that Access Hollywood video with Billy Bush..."

"One day," I said, "Trump will be under house arrest with that electronic ankle bracelet."

We were in agreement but the verbal ping pong petered out.

"Have you heard from your sister?"

"No."

"I'm getting worried. This is week two."

"Ariel's like street cats. They fall off roofs but land on their feet without a bruise."

"How often does she text you?" I asked.

"Not much."

He then looked at his phone and read the weather. We were in for a short heat wave, Santa Ana desert wind conditions.

"Are you zeroing in on your college choices?"

"More or less."

"A few UCs. A few Cal States. Some far away."

"Is this about what schools your friends choose?"

"No. I want a new set of friends next year."

"You have letters of recommendation?"

"Two teachers from last year. English and History."

"Good."

"Letters don't really get read, you know."

"Just in case."

"Yeah."

"Your grades are looking better."

"I know."

"It was hard the year after Mom died."

"You bet." he said quietly.

"Put that into your statement letter."

"I can't, Dad. It's whiny shit."

"Suit yourself."

"I probably want to be two or three hours from here."

"Fine, Barry. We can visit any campus."

"How long do we have to keep the cat?"

"Another week. Maybe two."

"Good."

"Ariel likes cats." I said.

We had a moment of silence.

"I'm not cleaning the litter."

"I didn't ask you to."

"Did you know that cleaning cat litter can lead to Toxoplasmosis? Which triggers rage in humans?

"No. I didn't know that, Barry."

"Cat shit can carry the Toxoplasmosis parasite."

On that note, Barry had disappeared. I brewed more coffee, read the newspaper, and then went for a jog around the neighborhood. My apprehensions this week were taking me to unwarranted moods. The High Holy Days hadn't fortified me as in past years. The month was spiralling wicked little sparks. It seemed that my use to others appeared mechanical like a kitchen appliance. Yom Kippur emphasized life ahead should be a devotion to repair the sins of yesteryear. Big and little sins, visible sins and less visible sins. Our origins began with hope, yet theologians claimed we began with original sin.

Nonetheless, Benny's late-night phone call was slow moving poison in my psyche. He may have thought he was being candid and reverent with personal history, but it left a residue of shame. I thought I knew my father quite well. He carried on with a moral compass. Could my father have been so proficient an actor to keep his darker profile from view? If only the family which Traci and I created were whole today, such toxin would be ineffectual.

CHAPTER FOURTEEN

Thursday morning I had arranged for one of my graduate students, Colby, to foster Cassandra for the next six months. Colby loved animals and he had cats growing up in Boston. Colby's large studio apartment was near campus, his lease allowed small pets with a two-hundred-dollar damage deposit, and a temporary cat was perfect for his lifestyle. Because he travelled often for his dissertation research, he avoided acquiring a pet. That was what he told me over the phone. I attested that Cassandra, although equipped with claws, had not scratched any furniture in my home. I offered to buy a large cat tree or scratching post to provide positive alternatives. I promised Colby three thousand dollars for his trouble this academic year and I guaranteed to replace any furniture, any area rug, or any electronic equipment damaged by Cassandra. Colby was gracious in accepting the cat, the cash, and the trust.

I told Colby half truths about Cassandra's origins. Yes, Cassandra came from New York and was kept by an elderly gentleman named Benny who was practically my uncle. Cassandra's owner had lapsed into more dementia and, during my visit east, I decided to rehome Cassandra rather than take the cat to a shelter. If Colby could take a photo of Cassandra every other day on some furniture, or by the window, or chewing on a potted plant on the kitchen table, I would then send it to Benny's caregiver in New York. This would lift Benny's depression, I had said. Colby would be told by April what Benny's immediate family might wish to do about the cat. Maybe Cassandra would return to New York. I shared with Colby that Barry's asthma made cat care something to avoid at our home. Barry doesn't have asthma, so that was another lie about the situation. I also joked that after I saw the movie *Cats* on the flight back to California, I've been having nightmares about felines. Colby laughed politely.

That morning I drove to Colby's apartment with Cassandra in the cat carrier. I was getting practiced at animal transport. Because I tried to be thorough, I purchased a few days ago on Amazon a name tag and collar for Cassandra. The ID had her name and my cell phone number. In the unlikely event that the cat got out, there could be some safeguard of return.

Colby, with his sleek cloth mask emblazoned with Joe Biden's campaign logo, helped me transfer stuff from my car. I carried the cat, a sack of Petco cat toys, and a large package of kibble. Colby handled the cat litter with a very fancy roof attachment and a fourteen-pound Clump & Seal Multi-Cat Scented Clay Litter. Colby said that Cassandra was pretty and he trusted this to be the start of a wonderful friendship. I gave Colby cash in an envelope, crisp Benjamins from the bank. Anytime Colby had to be away for a few days, I offered to drop by and feed Cassandra. Colby's dissertation was on the screenwriting of François Truffaut and I was one of his advisors. Conversations with Colby were gratifying and his writing was simply superb. He had a unique window into Truffaut's canon. My faith about Cassandra's new foster home was of the highest order. I took Cassandra out of the cat carrier, hugged her, and set her gently on the plush carpet of Colby's living room. Colby and I bumped elbows in lieu of a handshake, and I got back to my car. The morning was off to a good start after some arduous days.

During the drive back home, I owned yet another Yom Kippur revelation. I was an angry man. I acknowledged that. I had a running complaint against God in the last few years, which I had repressed with success. Traci was killed by God, not by pancreatic cancer. I had blamed God for stealing my wife. I had blamed God for hurting our daughter and son. I had blamed God for losing my faith and my instinct to love. I had tempered this long-seeded unconscious blame by constructing an evolving spiritual contract. I had coached myself to devote love and energy to our surviving family. I had reinforced that idea with analogues to other families pained by death, excruciating illnesses, and economic distress. I had returned to dusty books by Kierkegaard for inner conviction, *Fear and Trembling* and *Either/Or*. I had plowed all of my being into the Danish philosopher's knight of faith – an individual who is able to embrace mortal life, found in *Either/Or*:

> When around one everything has become silent, solemn as a clear, starlit night, when the soul comes to be alone in the whole world, then before one there appears, not an extraordinary human being, but the eternal power itself, then the heavens open, and the I chooses itself or, more correctly, receives itself. Then the personality receives the accolade of knighthood that ennobles it for an eternity.

Kierkegaard had positioned Job in several of his works, from *Repetition* to *Fear and Trembling*, as a figure crushed to the bone and not prepared for any restitution. One of the paradoxes of Job persuaded me – in the year after Traci's passing – that Job's silence could be comprehended as the purest language of human suffering. Job sublimated the endless torment without having a bible studies 'Job' at his disposal. We apply Job's fate as a learning model. This was always too cerebral for my pain after Traci passed away. Making this adhere with efficacy meant fabricating a solemn vow. It was a secret vow of stoicism. This spiritual construction secured my ability to function. In this COVID year of hell, I knew that my skepticism and bitterness were massive hurdles.

If Traci were alive and saw my inner bitterness, she would let me have private space. She wouldn't pry. She would be physical. She would touch the back of my neck. She would hug me as I fell asleep. This was something that cannot be outsourced to another. If I were to mention Kierkegaard to Traci, she would laugh in my face calling me an asshole and teasing my absurdities. Her laughter was music. Atonement, to Traci, was a dusty, ridiculous idea. If I were allowed to have died the moment Traci had died, we would have had spiritual unity. But I had survived her. I tried to take care of our teenage offspring. I was not perfect at this. She would say to me there was nothing to atone. She would say that we are human. Only the gods have to atone. She would refer to divinity as the gods.

At noon I received a phone call from Gerhardt's wife Jackie. She gave me a long, convoluted speech about her husband's crisis and their marriage rupture. The rawness of this call was fingernails on a school blackboard. Jackie and I weren't very conversant over the years. She told me that her father was seriously sick in Akron, Ohio and he lived alone. She thought I already knew their marriage was in turmoil. I told her this was news to me. Jackie hoped that I would spare Oscar from disaster. Saving his career had nothing to do with saving the marriage. Jackie knew of his pattern with younger women on campus. She planned to leave for Ohio by the end of the week, leaving Oscar alone with the family Golden Retriever. Jackie refused to get off the phone until I promised to make Oscar's circumstances better at school.

"I have no impact on how this will play out." I said softly.

"Jonathan, you can stand up for him."

"I already talked to the department chair."

"Talk to the dean."

"I'll talk to the dean. Jackie, I have to get off this call and get to another appointment."

"You know he suffers from Tourette syndrome?"

"I didn't know."

"Campus should know that Tourette is a mitigating factor. You've seen Oscar's shoulder twitch . . . his foul language, his repetitive phrases when he's stressed."

"Don't we all do that, Jackie?"

"Damn it, Jonathan. I'm serious about his condition."

"Is Tourette in his health file at campus?"

"I'm certain he disclosed his condition at the time of hire."

"Fine, Jackie. This might help. Oscar can make this known to the inquiry."

We were making headway in her view.

"Tourette is his best defense, but he's reluctant to blame the illness. You can tell Horowitz to document this condition." she said.

"I'll remind Horowitz today." I said.

There was a silence.

"He's one of your closest friends, goddamnit. He would take a bullet for you."

And so it went. She made it clear that her marriage to Oscar was failing and she was making the best of a bad situation.

"I'll stay in touch with Oscar every other day until this smooths out."

"You might try reaching the Chancellor too. I've heard you have a good relationship with him."

She gave me her cell phone number. The call ended. Who else would lobby for him – his daughter Penelope at Oberlin?

I read the Google docs in the department shared drive in preparation for the second faculty meeting of the week. The department and the entire arts and humanities division were forced to make blueprints to reduce our operational budget in a fluid retrenchment. This had come on the heels of last spring's financial reduction with the onset of COVID and the vacuuming of our department's carryforward funds by upper administration. Campus was morphing into a corporation. All of which could be underscored by the indelicate question: which limb next to amputate? Should we lose critical staff and adjunct faculty who worked on campus for years? These were people who had depended on the university to be decent.

The Google docs outlined how to overhaul our faculty governance org chart. The goal was to reduce the powers ostensibly of our dean and chair but yet not hold any individual accountable for our financial future. We would exalt our students to full voting status on policies despite Senate Faculty rules. We would reduce the size of the graduate program and forfeit the opportunities of postdocs. Invariably these actions would impact teaching assistants' support towards undergraduate classes. We would end buying and repairing faculty computers. We would eliminate travel funds for scholarly activity. Stipends and course relief incentives would vanish. We would thin out the catalogue of courses. Along with countless other campuses from coast to coast, Higher Education had moved closer to a fast food franchise economy.

All that would be left to do to continue this absurdity would be campus posting calories in the course catalogue.

My iPhone pinged with a text from Yunmei. She didn't think Columbia could help her and she tried to reach an official at the university getting an appointment ten days away. Yunmei said her aunt from Shanghai was coming to get her. Yunmei distrusted this woman. Yunmei asked if I could wire her money. Her plan was to hide from her aunt and remain in New York at a hidden address. I texted back asking how much cash was needed. She was embarrassed and said I was too nice. Another text came, saying five thousand dollars would get her through the semester. She planned to move out of her shared, upscale apartment for one of Manhattan's YMCAs to save money. Her aunt wouldn't know about the change of address from Yunmei's two roommates.

I went out to the patio. I did offer to help her. Yunmei was calming down and not motivated to do anything harmful to the Chinese Consulate or to herself. I had never gifted money to a student in my teaching career. But these were extraordinary times. My bank app would permit me to send via Zelle someone twenty-five hundred dollars per day.

I texted Yunmei that I would send the money today and Friday, in two sums. Texting this made me feel strange. She might be able to prevail, dodging her mother's sister from Shanghai and continue her studies. The Beijing authorities who had Yunmei on their dashboard might refocus to other political miscreants. After all, the offense was mostly a one-off seen by a few thousand folks on the Internet.

Yunmei texted back.

Thank you. This is so generous. I will get better on all fronts. I love you for your kindness, Professor Klein.

This last sentence threw me for a loop.

Please stay safe Yunmei.

There were no more texts between us today. I logged into the faculty Zoom. For this meeting, I choose to post my profile photo in lieu of live video camera on me.

CHAPTER FIFTEEN

Thursday evening after Barry and I had dinner, I met Skip Lamont, a mercurial and overconfident friend from Philosophy, at BJ's Restaurant for drinks and appetizers. Over the years, we made a habit of meeting every few months. It was harder in the first chapter of the Coronavirus as we had attempted the Zoom happy hour concoction where it is impossible to clink glasses. Lamont was a mischievious political philosopher who loved to reinvigorate classic Marxism into the Black Lives Matter movement at small or large gatherings. Friends had trouble deciphering if he was genuinely pro BLM, in a time when it was unthinkable to stand apart from the movement. He defended BLM from the ridiculous Marxist aspersions coming out of the hard right, but he questioned BLM about its long term agenda. He argued for reparations to all African Americans and to cultural institutions that were solidly Black. Skip often told friends that someone removed his Black Lives Matter bumper stick while parking at the supermarket in La Jolla. Was his joke half true?

He quipped that he acquired his nickname because he jumped third grade from Montesorri preschool. Lamont had boasted that he could read Margaret Wise Brown's *Goodnight Moon* at the age of eighteen months and the complete works of Shakespeare before his seventh birthday. Lamont's mother told us years ago at his catered Christmas party that he got the name playing college basketball for the Minnesota Golden Gophers. Skip Lamont – tall, fair-haired, chin dimpled and lean, with a gaunt Max von Sydow expression – had cultivated an obnoxious, droll wit. He had a streak of charisma when he flicked the switch, which he claimed drove up his utility bills. We enjoyed one another's company in good or foul spirits, made each other laugh, took turns playing chief cynic or straight man, and supplied each other with insider campus dirt. Tonight over draft beer, Lamont criticized campus for misleading thousands of students to pay premium for dorms in a year doomed to be online schooling. It wasn't his Marxist critique per se, but the blunt bullshit sophistry one might hear on evening Fox News or MSNBC's *Morning Joe*.

Lamont did extend sympathy to the university fiscal leadership for an impossible situation. He had predicted that twenty percent of the private colleges in our country would either collapse or be acquired by predator schools at the end of the Coronavirus era. He went on to predict that a robust liberal arts education would be a relic of our generation. He bemoaned the fact that we were brutally undermining Pell Grant students – those who came from families with income under fifty thousand dollars. Our campus had many more Pell Grants five years ago, but now students were sporting BMWs and parking illegally in faculty spots. These affluent kids, taking the seats of Pell students, didn't worry about parking tickets. Lamont's other projection which was unsurprising, faulted America's rising dependency on Chinese internationals to continue to pay full freight as rich non-residents. This trend would be a jolt to many Research 1 public institutions as they lose sizable international enrollments, on the heels of government funding cuts, dwindling student housing and parking fees.

Lamont praised MIT and Harvard for pioneering open, no-cost, online courses years before the COVID fiasco. He gave a solid compliment to Starbucks for granting employees a modified free college education at Arizona State their last two years of a baccalaureate, assuming employees had community college credits prior to coming to Starbucks. Lamont, in the same breath, had disapproved of the term *barista* – for rhyming with Sandinista. This was Lamont saluting online instruction which normally would take a college years to develop, but the virus pushed the nation to prepare remote classrooms in a fortnight. I believed that these virtual classrooms had opened Pandora's Box, shortchanging the intrinsic qualities of being in a room with an educator. His central argument was twofold about mass produced baccalaureates: degrees were too expensive putting students into eternal debt, and high schools had prepared teenagers with uncreative, imbecilic platforms for abstract university learning. Our colleges and universities perpetuated this human farming system, knowing their eroding economics. Students today were programmed for rote memory, faculty fawning, and cheap mechanics to earn top grades. Even superior students had trouble composing salient, organized six-page papers in MLA format. Many padded their essays with extraneous quotations triple spaced and Adobe software graphics.

Lamont gossiped about the reports of some elite in the Chancellor's cabinet hounded by a group lawsuit citing gender abuse, hot tub parties, marijuana and alcohol abuse. The worst of these unfounded stories suggested that the Chancellor knew and was an enabler, enhancing the negative atmosphere. Lamont delighted in the entertainment value of these rumors, providing an endless source of dirty jokes. Lamont thought the scandals as comparable to Liberty University's President Jerry Falwell Jr. – pool boy sex with Falwell's wife while Falwell watched in the corner of his bedroom. Lamont guessed that there would be a large settlement but the media would never get wind of anything. Lamont praised campus counsel for adroit damage control. Most of Lamont's barbs were aimed at COVID safety measures on campus that were becoming ineffectual. Testing dorms' wastewater was an inexpensive Yale idea assuming sewage predicts the COVID cases faster than voluntary student testing. Lamont believed that weekly campus testing could turn the corner, but monthly intervals insufficient to stem the spread. More to the point, how do you chain students to the campus on the weekend? How do you prevent them from partying in a room? He expected our campus to reduce tuition by one third, move everyone out of the dorms by Halloween with a full housing refund, and half our general education requirements to hasten graduation until the virus vanishes. Lamont would love to banish the high salaried administrative officers and redirect all governance to faculty, students and alumni. He lamented that for the newly minted doctorates there would be no jobs in higher education. His last prediction, during our third beer, was that tenure will disappear from coast to coast by 2030. "Throw the bums out." he chortled.

I gave Lamont no counterargument. My mind was preoccupied by Gerhardt's fate. When Lamont resorted to his favorite bromide about Marxist philosopher Herbert Marcuse in San Diego during the late 1960s battling Governor Ronald Reagan, I was ready to leave BJ's.

"What's eating you?" asked Lamont.

"Nothing."

"Did a publisher drop you?"

"No."

"Problems with your kids?"

"No."

"Gerhardt's mess?"

"What do you know?"

"Gerhardt's down for the count, Jonathan."

"He has Tourette Syndrome." I said.

"Oscar needs a fucking good attorney or a voodoo doll."

"He's a good friend, Skip."

"Tourette's not a secure defense."

Lamont laughed with a little bit of conscience.

"He's near retirement age, so it's time for him to buy a good set of Callaway golf clubs."

"He doesn't play."

"Golf's one of the best things to do before dying, Jonathan. We look for lost balls."

"Gerhardt doesn't have self-esteem to get through this."

"And if not golf, there is always watercolor class at the Y."

"You don't care about his fall."

"Look, students are off limits."

"You and I know colleagues who go to student parties and get high with their students."

"Yes." Lamont agreed. "And they keep their hands to themselves."

"His wife is leaving him."

"How do you know?"

"She told me over the phone."

"You're right in the middle of this soap opera?"

"I am."

"If I were Gerhardt, I'd rush the dean to negotiate early retirement. Avoid the campus investigation and grab a position at a third-tier institution in Montana. He is a 'leading scholar' on the graphic novel." he added with a flipped tongue.

"So much for your compassionate Marxism."

"Marxists negotiate all the time."

The waiter came over informing us that BJ's would be closing in ten minutes.

"I want to compliment the chef," went on Lamont, "for these avocado spring rolls are truly gourmet pleasures."

The waiter, masked, smiled with his eyes, nodded, and glided off to another table.

"I recommend Gerhardt buy a rowing machine, stow it in the garage, row an hour a day. That's what I did during the start of quarantine. I watched sea movies on my iPad next to the rower. It's perfect. *Titanic, The Perfect Storm, The Poseidon Adventure, The Life Aquatic*..."

Lamont picked up the check. We walked into the parking lot.

"Jonathan, to this day I can't figure out why you devoted your career to film studies. It's a field of tortured pretenders and bottom feeders. A tide pool of barnacles. You would have been a brilliant philosophy theorist. I'm certain that you had a destructive influence at college. How the universe ruins young talent. At least you steered clear of theatre and performance studies which are the lowest of the low. Drama departments are so self-indulgent, more woke than *Mother Jones*, and as *farblondzhet* as Dante's ninth circle of Inferno."

"You've picked up some more Yiddish." I said.

Lamont laughed as he put on his face mask and reached to give me his trademark bear hug. I stepped back, thinking we should have some virus caution. He then got into his Tesla and drove away.

I forgot where I parked my car. My phone inside my coat pocket buzzed with a text. It was Colby who had texted two photos of Cassandra. One photo was the cat drinking out of the toilet. Ten minutes later I found my car.

As I drove home, I thought I caught a glimpse of Ariel's black Honda Civic a block from the house. I asked Barry if indeed Ariel had come by.

"Yeah." he said.

"Really. What did she say?"

"Nothing. She just ran in and grabbed more clothes."

"That was it?"

"You two didn't talk?"

"No. She was in a hurry."

"How did she look?"

"A little messy."

"Oh."

"I just went back into my room."

"Was she alone?"

"Yeah. But somebody was in the car."

"You don't know who?"

"No."

"Did she ask for money?"

"Yeah."

"Did you give her any?"

"I had two fives. I gave her one."

"Okay."

"Anything else, Dad?"

"Set your alarm for school. Sleep well."

"Good night." his door closed as though by an invisible hand.

I tried to reach Ariel on the phone but she didn't pick up. I hurried to my car and drove around the neighborhood on the chance I would see her Honda Civic. This escapade went on for twenty minutes. I finally parked the car and took a shower, washing away a feeling of inadequacy and emptiness. Before going to bed, I had an impulse to check my black shoebox under the blankets in my closet. The box was opened. Ariel had taken the spare cash.

CHAPTER SIXTEEN

I had completed the proofing of my last chapter for Michigan Press and emailed them the manuscript Friday afternoon. This felt comforting. Getting some distance on the material I could see that the new pages were equal in quality and weight to the rest of the manuscript. I was certain there would be a slew of minor notes and some larger, workable concerns. For all I cared, Michigan was free to retitle the book if it pleased their editorial team. The branding and marketing of the edition was a tertiary issue. In my detachment was a sense of broader freedom.

That afternoon I did online research concerning Tourette Syndrome and the misconceptions about this illness. It's untrue that those with Tourette's disorder fall into obscene words and gestures. It's untrue that those with Tourette's will erupt with explosive anger often, have alcohol or drug problems, and suffer repetitive facial or body tics. Tourette Syndrome was not linked to sexual harassment and predatory behavior, but was associated with failed social decision-making actions governing a wide range of practical life. If Jackie proceeded with this defense, the chances were not very promising for her husband. However, I was more sympathetic to him knowing about the disorder.

I asked my son mid-afternoon if he had plans for the weekend.

"No."

"Whenever you go out, you wear a mask?"

"Yeah, of course."

"How about a kayak rental in the bay?"

"No."

"Golf? Eighteen holes or miniature?"

"No."

"Cycling to Coronado, take the ferry with bikes?"

"No."

"Rob a bank? Flee to Mexico?"

"No."

"Can't get you to laugh, not for all the wine in Sonoma."

Barry smiled with some effort.

"Did you notice the cat's gone?"

"Yes."

"Want to know what happened?"

"You sold the cat on Craigslist?"

"One of my grad students volunteered."

"Lucky us." he said still focused on a desktop game.

"Something's on your mind, Barry."

"I don't know."

"I sense it."

I sat on his unmade bed.

"I hate online classes. It's a pain in the ass."

"I know. I'm sorry."

"I'll get through it. Don't worry."

"Do you think about Mom a lot?"

"Sometimes."

"Would it be different if she were alive?"

"There'd still be online school."

"You know what I mean."

"She's not here."

"I think it would be better." I said.

"Dad, it wasn't all that good."

"What do you mean?"

"I don't know if this is something to say."

"Say it. Go ahead."

"It's going to hurt you."

"How do you know?"

"I know."

He paused his computer game and scratched around his ankles.

"I've a few flea bites from the cat."

"I'm sorry, Barry."

"Mom wasn't completely in love with you."

This was something too strange to hear from Barry.

"How do you know?"

"I kind of know. Leave it at that."

"I can't leave it at that. Did she say something to you?"

"Not exactly."

"Then what?"

"When you were away for academic conferences, she had a special friend."

"A special friend?"

"Dad, she was seeing someone. Okay?"

"You're not making this up?"

"I'm not making this up."

Silence and more silence.

"Who was he?"

"Dad..."

"Tell me, goddamnit."

"It won't bring her back."

"Do I know this person?"

"Yes, sort of."

"Who is he?"

"It's not a he."

I found myself leaning back on his bed and banging my head against the wall.

"Who?"

"One of her girlfriends from the dog park. Theresa. With the Alaskan Malamute."

"Theresa?"

"Yeah."

"Did Mom know that you knew?"

"Yeah, I think she knew."

Our family had a chocolate lab – Rocket – who had died eighteen months before Traci's death. We had rescued the lab while he was an older pup. There was a history of abuse, we were led to believe. Rocket was very shy and hard to read. Traci was the primary caregiver for Rocket. He was basically a good, spirited dog with a food guarding problem.

"I'm beyond words."

"Yeah. I can see."

"Did Theresa sleep over while I was away?"

Barry nodded his head.

"Ariel knows?"

"Yeah, of course."

"Anything else I should know, Barry?"

My son shook his head and expressed empathy with his eyes.

"Mom always loved you . . . at times it just wasn't completely."

With this news bouncing wildly inside me, I had to take a long walk outside. Clearly I was processing awful things. Why did Barry tell me this today? Why didn't he bring this up years ago? How could this be true and how could I be this clueless? Was I sleepwalking in the last years of marriage? What was it that Traci needed from someone else? And why Theresa from the fucking dog park? Ignorance would have been bliss.

I walked for an hour unable to think. I was fighting my rage. Then came several pings on my cell. Colby texted me concerned that the cat was coughing up fur balls and Colby was worried that Cassandra might have the virus. Benny texted news that he was running a high fever and he wanted me to phone him over the weekend. He added that another Atria resident came down with COVID and Benny was just tested again. Gerhardt texted to say that he was still expecting my support. He added that Jackie flew to Ohio before dinner which lit his fuse.

I expected to hear from Yunmei as well. Perhaps news of her aunt's arrival and meeting her at the Harlem YMCA residency desk. Or learning that Yunmei got arrested by New York City Police near the Chinese Consulate. But there came no message from Yunmei. No acknowledgement of the second Zelle transfer of twenty-five hundred dollars. I grew worried that something had happened to her. Worrying about atypical students like Yunmei was my neurosis.

In Marcel Proust's *In Search of Lost Time* (*À la recherche du temps perdu*), Proust's avatar and neurotic narrator Marcel decided to become an author and describes in excessive detail what he saw. He inadvertently approached a window at composer Vinteuil's house. Vinteuil had died heartbroken after his young daughter fell in love with a woman. Marcel observed the two lovers as they mock Vinteuil's memory and Marcel was very bothered by this – as if he, Marcel, had projected himself into Vinteuil's being. Likewise, Marcel Proust had injected himself into his semi-autobiographical Marcel for a therapeutic purpose? Where was truth amidst the fictional confessional?

Thinking of Proust's self-absorptions, I was listening to the Bill Evans Trio's *Jade Vision* – the bass so distinctive at the start, theme and pulse so elusive, other worldly, and unsentimental. I was buffering myself, while over the music Barry's words about Traci filled my head. I was flooded by my own pain and ignorance.

I saw neighbors, masked, outside their homes. I saw neighbors walking in pairs. I saw dog walkers and kids on bikes. In the twilight I saw a fleeting coyote where the property line of one house skirts the canyon rim. Coyote sightings were rare. I saw clearly Traci's beatific face the day we were married.

I reentered my home. It was getting dark and the wind was kicking up. Only Barry's room lights were on. I poured myself a single malt whiskey. I drank slowly as I turned on some lamps in the living room and den. I went into the office to feed Cassandra. I filled a bowl of water and then spilled some on my trousers. I was aware that I was now on autopilot and missing the cat.

The last ten days lingered. Images arose of my mother's grave forming semiotic unconscious memories of New York to California, of Rosh Hashanah to Yom Kippur, of Horowitz and Gerhardt, of Yunmei and Chinese authorities, between aged Benny and young Barry. And then imaginary images of Traci in her denim jacket with silver studs together with her heavyset lover Theresa, inside the chain link fenced dirty dog park.

CHAPTER SEVENTEEN

Last night brought about twisted sleep with dreams that I only half recalled. There was a wedding scene. My daughter in a white dress. Or was this Yunmei? Seeing the bride from behind at a far distance, a glimpse of dark lush hair. I was in black tie and uncomfortably dressed. Something was wrong. My attire was ripping. My tuxedo jacket? Was this Ariel's fantasy wedding? People in attendance were not recognizable. Where was the groom? There was a long line of cars outside a fancy white structure. Valets were running about like firefighters. Management suddenly informed guests to evacuate what seemed to be the ballroom. The crowd acted unruly. Chaos ensued. Police vans and fire trucks were in the parking lot. I had trouble recalling other details. There were California wildfires after a historic summer season of flame. Or was this dream about our world ablaze?

In today's email was Michigan Press' acknowledgment of getting the manuscript and a sentence of appreciation. There was a long letter from Celeste which I didn't wish to read until later in the day. When her letters were voluminous, I involuntarily sped through. Best not skim her email. The New York Times headlines were blunt about the explosive social justice protests in multiple cities. Barry was still asleep. I left him a note saying that I would be back by nine, having gone for a bike ride.

More often than not, I listened to an audio book while bicycling but today my attention span was thin. My conversation with Barry left a residue. I had determined that he was trying to help me with the facts and with mourning. Barry was never cruel to me. It was likely that in his conveyance, Barry was freeing himself of being a witness to Theresa. The reversal of our father/son dynamics had been unnerving. A parent should be the one to tell his child about a complicated truth, rather than the inverse. For over two years I was mindful of Barry's misfiring energies in high school. It was as though Barry perceived the future – his future – as a ridiculous goal. His morose thinking was palpable. It didn't come from reading Albert Camus or Hunter S. Thompson or even all the *Diary of a Wimpy Kid* books Barry had collected and loved. He evaluated his boring courses as useless material never to be needed. From the end of middle school into the first semesters of high school, he was conserving his intellectual efforts taking shortcuts whenever possible. He stopped reading.

Barry's remarkable academic conversion began with a new guidance counselor, Mrs. Sandoval, who closely resembled Jennifer Lopez – JLO. Mrs. Sandoval created her own intervention, slapping Barry into a harsh reality where high school ended and a lifelong job at a hamburger drive-thru began.

"In March of your senior year," she had said, "when your friends open letters of college acceptances you'll be whistling into your metal school locker."

I was present for the intervention. Complicating the wastefulness of Barry's academic self-sabotage, he was a GATE seminar student as he entered third grade. GATE students were selected using an assessment called the Raven test, similar to an IQ test, mostly comprised of abstract reasoning. In our school district, Barry was clustered with other GATE students through elementary and middle school, and propelled into high school advance placement. Some GATE kids find school boring but nearly always maintain high grades. The incongruity of Barry's annual academic trajectory was his pattern of beginning each school year brilliantly only to crash by November.

Perhaps a factor in Barry's instability was the fact that he accelerated a grade when he began public school. Throughout his school seasons, Barry's physical growth proved late compared to the standard pediatric growth charts. When he had entered high school his height was closer to a boy age twelve. Teen confidence was not strong. But in

the summer between tenth and eleventh grade, he experienced a wonderful growth spurt which was a godsend. Obviously, Traci missed the
satisfaction of seeing him transform into a young handsome man.

As I made Barry's Saturday breakfast, I had flashbacks of the funeral
service for Traci. I tried to recall those who came to pay their respects.
Traci's extended family members were present, her colleagues from
the university library were there, her friends from the city and the
state were there. I vaguely remember that Theresa was part of the
community in attendance. Theresa was nearly invisible all through the
service. I felt pained this morning conjuring the dog park queen.

Barry in bottom pajamas and no top came into the kitchen. His
thick hair was brushed neatly. I admired his personal grooming from
his neck up. He said good morning and I asked how hungry was he. He
requested two eggs, two waffles, two strips of very lean bacon – over
cooked was *de rigueur*. We adhered to the routine. He did ask if there
were any cold Starbucks' Frappuccinos and fortunately one bottle was
left in the fridge behind the dill pickle jar.

I left him to his privacy in the kitchen and remembered to go
into the garage to close the rolling metal door. My bicycle was still
in the driveway. The front yard appeared fake to me. Roses in bloom
looked surreal. The grass was healthy, the lawn as green as a ballad
of Ireland.

My phone rang as I was cleaning up the kitchen. It was a starburst
of voice, Celeste.

"Did I wake you, Jonathan?"

"Nope. How's your weekend?"

"It could be better but the day is young." she said.

"Are you working today?"

"No. I need a real Saturday for me."

"What's the latest with Tony?"

"Didn't you get my email last night?"

"I did. I hadn't read it carefully when I opened it at night…"

"Well, read the damn email."

"Now?"

"Not now, I'm on the phone."

"Things aren't great in San Diego."

"Is COVID spiking in your county?"

"I haven't been checking the newspaper. Barry hit me with some family news."

"Want to tell me about it?"

"Not really, Celeste. I need to process things he said."

"I've my flight dates to L.A. and you can find them in the email."

"Good."

"I'm flying business class. Safer than coach."

"Still the same cabin air, bathroom surfaces, airport gates...you don't have the antibodies."

"Actually I do have the antibodies. I was just tested."

"Great."

A brief silence.

"Well, my calendar is wide open." I said.

"Okay. I can either get a hotel or you can be my Airbnb."

"A hotel might be wiser, with my son at home."

"You said he was eighteen."

"He's seventeen. And has a loud snore."

Celeste laughed.

"So do you. A hotel is probably better. Look Jonathan, I'm feeling happy that Tony's moved his things."

"Are you talking to lawyers?"

"Yeah. I'm not concerned about the court maneuvers. I'll come out just fine. But I'm more concerned that this fat fuck cretin in the White House, losing the election but no peaceful exit."

"Chief Justice Roberts will address the nation if Trump drags his bone spurs."

"Dream on. No one in the Federal Government has the balls to do a proper eviction."

"Hope for a miracle."

"Trump can stir up a goddamn riot to divert the transition. Mark my words. Did I tell you that Tony dined with him at Mar-a-Lago in 2013? It was a party for twenty white rich idiots with checkbooks in hand. Tony has a framed photo with Trump."

"Why did you mention an abortion last week?"

"My therapist prompted it."

"But for a result, or for your therapy?"

"Isn't that one and the same thing, Jonathan?"

"For a result, you were aiming at me."

"Of course, I was aiming at you. I love you, you colossal moron."

"I would have urged you not to abort."

"That's you talking in 2020. The year the globe fell off its axis. I fell in love with you for good reasons."

"Celeste, I fell in love with you just as hard."

"I want to believe you."

"What made you mention the abortion?"

"I thought I had a second chance with you."

"I'm sorry we didn't bring a child into the world together."

"I'm just as sorry, Jonathan."

We heard each other breathing softly.

"Your son will soon be off to college. I'm not bitter. I'm happy for Barry and for you."

"Yes. Thank you."

"We'll see each other soon."

"Yes. Soon." I said slowly.

CHAPTER EIGHTEEN

In bed preparing for restless sleep, I imagined Celeste wanting a longer conversation about our life together if we could time travel to younger selves. She was transparent, vulnerable and easy to understand over the phone. She might not realize that my optimism was in short supply, my resilience far from regenerating. Fate had little to do with anything, although I respected her concept of destiny. We matched each other as New Yorkers with our cocktail of arrogance, contradiction, and raucous insecurity. When things were good, we had romantic highs better than drugs. We knew how to tease each other to delight an erotic idea. Her unfolding disaster with Tony DeRosa could be sung as a sardonic country tune by Dolly Parton or "Weird Al" Yankovic.

I realized that Celeste viewed me differently and more gently in the aftermath of Traci's death, just as I saw that Celeste had been transformed in her second failed marriage. She was still very attractive and her rambunctious, rogue personality complemented my recesses.

Half asleep, I heard Traci's upper register voice as if she were leaving a recorded message. She implored me to erase Barry's assumptions about Theresa. Traci's imaginary voice pressed me to find Ariel before something terrible happened to her. Did I really hear Traci putting coded words together suggesting death was not a barrier. Did she say that the wall of our vanity made the afterlife beyond reach. One need not hire a séance conductor or a convincing charlatan. The dead spoke to us when we are very alone. In the first year after her passing,

I thought this was more true than not. This was how I perceived her beautiful voice.

Half asleep, I saw my aged mother at her Jewish Community Center during the festive holiday of Purim, children in costumes and volunteers at the gaming booths handing out carnival prizes tickets. Queen Esther was part of the Purim tale and a variation of my mother's name Essie. Children in costumes loved surprising their grandparents at Purim. The Jewish elderly quietly count on two hands how many more Purims lie ahead.

Half asleep, I dream of Yunmei and Ariel meeting in California. How they met, I have no idea. They talked energetically about clothing, music, freedom, and food. They discussed family and men. Yunmei expressed envy about Ariel having a sibling and about having more liberties as an American. Ariel showed Yunmei her TikTok lip sync skewering Ariana Grande. Yunmei responded saying China owns TikTok. Ariel and Yunmei agreed to take the pandemic vaccine once it clears clinical trials. Ariel gave Yunmei a makeover with mascara, lip liner, and unnatural hair coloring. They both laughed, saying a painted doll will always be a painted doll.

Half asleep, I held another premonition about Gerhardt.

My phone rang. Waking out of this half sleep, I didn't bother to screen the call.

"Hello?"

"Jonathan Klein?" The voice was gravel over a belt sander.

"Yes."

"This is Max Edelmann. Benny's son."

"Hello Max."

"What a lousy connection. Can you hear me?"

"Yes."

"We never met but I know you saw my father the other week."

"Actually, we met once at a large family event. Twenty-five years ago. Your cousin's wedding in Short Hills, New Jersey."

"No shit? I don't remember that. Sorry to wake you. You're on the immediate contact list my father compiled."

"What happened?"

"He was admitted to North Shore University Hospital ten hours ago. Benny has excessive fluid buildup in his lungs and the hospital thinks it's COVID."

"That's horrible, Max. I'm so sorry."

"Since he had pneumonia in 2017, the hospital is very concerned."

"I understand."

"Dad's eighty-two. Vital signs could be better. Oxygen level down."

"Is he on a ventilator?"

"No."

"That's good."

I heard Max Edelmann's heavy breathing.

"He said you have the cat."

"That's right."

"I can't hear you."

"That's right. I have Cassandra."

"Why the fuck do you have his cat?"

"Benny said that he wasn't allowed to keep the cat at Atria and that you were allergic to cats."

"That's bullshit. Atria has a two-pet maximum policy."

"That's what Benny told me, Max."

"And I'm not allergic to cats."

"Maybe Benny got confused?"

"I doubt it. My father's mind is sharp as a tack."

"Yes, your father's very quick."

There was a hole in our dialogue. My fatigue at this odd hour was obvious. Max's time zone was 4:00am. How shitfaced was he to phone me so late?

"So what's the deal with you and my father?"

"No deal. Your father gave a large loan to my father years ago."

"So?"

"So your father made a point about that to me."

"Are you hustling my father?"

"No."

"Was it a business loan?"

"Yeah. A car dealership. Can I call you tomorrow?"

"Your father sold Chevys?"

"Yeah."

"They're shitty cars."

"Nothing wrong with Chevys." I said mechanically.

"Why the fuck would my father stake money on a Chevrolet dealership?"

"It's really late, Max. Could we talk tomorrow?"

"Was your father blackmailing Benny?" he asked.

"No, that's crazy."

"Are you blackmailing my father?"

"No. Get off this subject."

"A few guys tried to blackmail him. He had them killed, Klein."

There was stillness. Max's breathing grew heavily as if he had asthma.

"Klein…"

"What?"

"Tell me the work you do."

"I'm a college professor."

"What do you teach?"

I wanted to hang up.

"What the fuck do you teach?"

"Nanoengineering."

I couldn't resist fucking with him.

"What the hell is that?"

"Energy conversion design, nano pills for erectile dysfunction, better living through…nanoengineering."

"Fucking asshole…"

"Max, I'm hanging up. Talk to you tomorrow."

"Klein, don't you dare hang up. How's the cat?"

"The cat's fine."

"What's her name?"

"Cassandra, priestess of Apollo."

"Bring back the cat this week."

"Why?"

"Because I'm telling you to get on a fucking plane."

"I could ship Cassandra on one of the airlines. But I can't fly this week. I'm teaching every day."

"Call in sick. Get on a plane."

"I can't do that."

"I'll send you my address."

Max hung up.

I wished this were a nightmare. A moment later, Max texted me his address in Larchmont, New York. After turning off my phone, I fell fast asleep.

When I got up Monday, I tried to analyze why Benny lied to me. Or why Max was lying to me. Why power trip over a cat? I had to phone Atria to find out Benny's health status before doing anything. Max could be screwing with me. My cat arrangements only went through Benny.

There were two prominent emails on my phone. One from Yunmei and the other from Jason Horowitz. I opened her email first.

CHAPTER NINETEEN

Yunmei asked if we could talk tonight, but I taught Mondays 6–9pm. It would have to be an hour before class. She was unable to check into the Harlem YMCA, close to Columbia. She mentioned success with the West Side YMCA on West 63rd Street, and a confrontation with her aunt Min over the phone. The West Side Y was a historical structure with imported Spanish tile, steps from Lincoln Center and Central Park. She strategized it was better to speak to her aunt by phone rather than block her number altogether. Having vacated her correct Manhattan address, Yunmei did not feel comfortable completely shutting off family. She was determined to finish Columbia and find a way to stay as long as possible in the United States.

She described how terrifying her aunt came across over the phone. Her aunt threatened Yunmei with disinheritance and legal actions that were draconian. Yunmei's father was hospitalized for a heart attack and her mother was followed by the secret police. Min bought two business class seats for their flight to China, one seat designated for Yunmei.

Yunmei's updates were uncomfortable to take in. She wanted an immediate response.

Yunmei had always despised her aunt for her skewered attitude on freedom, privacy, sexual relations, and liberal culture outside China. Yunmei had a fixation on Min's facial features which were puppet-like, pulling an overweight body, animated by a shrill voice. Min wore no makeup and no jewelry. Min's shoes were working class orthopedic. Yunmei's email was long and referenced the graffiti attack last May against the Chinese Consulate in Canada's Calgary. This intimated that Yunmei wasn't over her thirst to assault the Chinese government. She was aligning herself with an underground group at Fudan University in Shanghai. There were sizable protests against the government last December at Fudan. The end of her email thanked me for the five thousand dollars and she asked that I delete all her emails and texts.

Jason Horowitz's email was convoluted like Yunmei's, but the gist of his note concerned Oscar Gerhardt missing two classes, not replying to email and texts, not answering his cell. Horowitz had been trying to reach him since last Friday morning and he made a point of Gerhardt's accustomed prompt replies. Horowitz alluded to Jackie Gerhardt's passionate email to the chair and the matter of Oscar's Tourette Syndrome. Further, Horowitz had received a disturbing email from Gerhardt Thursday, signaling Gerhardt was entering a self-destructive zone. Horowitz worried that Gerhardt's health was in the balance. Horowitz wanted to talk about all of this, but most of all he wanted me to drive to Gerhardt's home to witness his condition. If I cared about Gerhardt's health, I should make haste. Horowitz was the Patron Saint of the Punctilious. So I planned to check in on Oscar today.

I first called Colby about the cat. Cassandra wasn't coughing anything up in the last twenty-four hours. Her appetite was better. All was back to normal, as reported by Colby over the phone. The cat did scratch him once when he was trying to free her claws from the shag rug. No stitches needed, just a little band aid.

I followed with a call to Atria Assisted Living. Max Edelmann was telling the truth. Benny was hospitalized for COVID. All those who had contact with him should be tested and also go into immediate quarantine.

I then received a call from New Montefiore Cemetery.

"Mr. Klein?"

"Yes."

"This is Miriam Weiss from New Montefiore. I wanted to follow up with your report on your mother's gravesite. Is this a good time?"

"Yes. Go ahead."

"Our office might have emailed earlier. The hedges over your mother's grave are now balanced. The sides look perfectly respectable. You cannot see any holes or crevices. We took photos of the repaired grave."

"Thank you. Do you know how this started? The email your office sent mentioned sinkholes."

"More likely this was hedgehogs. Natural nuisances. This land was once a farm. We have no video cameras beyond the office headquarters so we will never know."

"When was the last vandalism at New Montefiore?"

"Once in a blue moon. But this is a Jewish cemetery. We are targeted. New Montefiore apologizes to you and your family for any undue upset. Do you want the photos emailed to you or sent by USPS?"

"Email is fine. Thank you."

I phoned Horowitz.

"Jason, it's Jonathan."

"Sorry to trouble you but the office staff and I think you should drive over to Oscar's home today. Did you read my entire email?"

"I did."

"Well, no need to repeat myself. If you don't want to go alone, I can join you."

"Don't you think that's violating his privacy?"

"Working for a university means losing a little privacy. He missed classes without calling the office. Heaven forbid he had a stroke or an accident in the shower. His wife is out of town."

"I'll drive to his home today."

"Thanks so much, Jonathan."

"Hoping nothing weird there."

"By the way, his wife asked to make certain the dog is fed and not sleeping in the yard."

I hung up. Horowitz should just drive over as a colleague to Gerhardt.

It was time to make my son breakfast. Barry had online classes today with an everchanging daily schedule. Rather than walking upstairs, I texted Barry saying his omelet was on the kitchen table.

I called North Shore Hospital in hopes of speaking to Benny. The hospital operator tried his room, but no one answered. I was then told by the operator that Mr. Edelmann was moved to ICU.

I went online to get an estimate to ship Cassandra to New York State. After a few minutes of filling out a data sheet on Animal Transportation Worldwide (ATW), door-to-door delivery was not inexpensive. Added in was a driver to get the cat to Max Edelmann with $5,000 in pet health protection, flea medication, and GPS tracking which brought the cost to $6,928.10. Moreover, a veterinary check-up would be required prior to travel. Bookings that did not have a two-week notice would have an Express Fee applied. Not cheap by the mile or by the hour.

After coffee and croissant, I showered and shaved. It was getting close to 10am. I phoned Gerhardt, but there was no pick up and his voicemail was full. I headed over to his house. Gerhardt's Audi sedan was parked awry on his driveway with one tire on the lawn. A bright lamp in his living room window was on, and the curtains were open. Three New York Times in blue plastic wrap were dotting his front steps. Certainly that was a sign. I picked up the Times and rang his door bell. I was surprised that Gerhardt's dog wasn't barking. I had a nauseating sensation. I rang the bell a second time. I knocked on the door. Nothing. I tried the door knob, but the door was locked. I walked back to the driveway to see if there were any open windows visible. I proceeded around the side to the yard's tall wooden gate which was unlocked. Gerhardt's neighbor in a pink terry robe was in her yard and noticed me.

"I'm Oscar's friend Jonathan."

"Oh. Hi." she said.

"Oscar's not answering his phone for a few days. And I know Jackie went to help her father in Ohio."

"He's away too." she said. "Oscar asked me to watch their dog Zorro."

"His car is in the driveway."

"I know. Maybe he took a cab to the airport."

"Did he say where he was going?"

"No. But he should be home today. Our dogs get along. It's no problem."

"Thanks." I said, still uncomfortable with the situation. I gave her my campus business card with my cell phone included in case Gerhardt had a longer absence.

"Oscar will have to take back the dog tomorrow. Our family's driving up to Orange County for the week."

Gerhardt's neighbor went into her house. My compulsion was to try Gerhardt's patio door. The door was locked. The adjacent living room window by the door was open. I popped the window screen with my car keys and climbed inside like a prowler. More lights were on which seemed incongruous in morning. I called out Oscar's name. The bathroom off the living room had a towel on the floor along the threshold. A bathroom light was on. I looked inside. The toilet was not flushed. Again, I called out Oscar's name. I was perspiring profusely.

I walked into Gerhardt's den and his office, and went upstairs to check the bedrooms. The first bedroom was his daughter's and her door was open. The room was spartan and orderly. I continued down the corridor to the next bedroom. The master bedroom door was partly open. I called out his name again. I waited. I pushed the door and entered.

Gerhardt, fully clothed, was lying inanimate on his bed. His antique night table lamp was on. His eyeglasses were on his ashen face. A half full glass of water sat on the night table, next to an empty whiskey glass. A bottle of Macallan was on the carpeted floor by the bed. On second glance I saw a prescription behind the box of tissues on the other night table. My heart was racing. I shook Gerhardt's shoulder and called out to him. His eyeglasses slipped off his nose. It looked like he wasn't breathing. I took his pulse. He had a weak pulse. I read the prescription label. It was generic Vicodin, 10 mg. and the container was empty. I immediately called 911.

CHAPTER TWENTY

I met the ambulance at the house. Gerhardt got to the hospital thirty minutes after the 911 call. The hospital pumped his stomach. The doctors feared that the window of time had passed to effectively extract the toxins. Further, Gerhardt had slipped into a coma. He was alive but his condition was critical. As they analyzed his blood, the hospital had a timeline on the pills, Tylenol, and whiskey.

In the hospital waiting room, my composure was barely holding up. I was praying that the doctors got him in the nick of time. Gerhardt was still alive. There were grounds for hope. Yet I was blaming myself for not checking right after Jackie's call. Assuming the hospital could save him, his apparent encephalopathy triggered by alcohol, hydrocodone bitartrate and acetaminophen could put him at risk for brain damage. The hospital staff encouraged me to go home. Hours had passed. I needed to phone Gerhardt's wife.

"Jackie, it's Jonathan."

"Hi Jonathan."

"There is very bad news. I'm at the hospital. Oscar's in a coma."

She was flabbergasted and the call dropped. She called me right back. I relayed to her how I found him. Jackie was stunned by the details and suddenly fell apart. She told me with embarrassment that Oscar had threatened to take his life several times. There was one occasion when he had passed out cold. He mixed painkillers with scotch whenever they had a turbulent fight.

"I'm praying to God." she said haltingly.

"The hospital has your phone number."

"Thank you."

"The doctors fear brain damage."

"Dear Jesus."

"I'm assuming you'll fly back immediately."

"Yes, of course. Once I get hired help for my father today, yes. By Wednesday evening."

"And Penelope?"

"I'll see her tomorrow. Oberlin's an hour from Akron."

She waited a few seconds and hung up. How far Ohio seemed.

I told the hospital that I reached Gerhardt's spouse who was arranging emergency care for her non-ambulatory father. The hospital needed to contact her regarding Gerhardt's life support protocols and wanted specifics from me about other next of kin. I only had Jackie's contact information.

I phoned Horowitz and left voicemail. I had a bitter taste in my mouth. My cloth face mask was soiled. I signed out of the hospital and had trouble in the cavernous garage finding my car. I questioned myself if I was fit to drive home.

Barry was in his room with Zoom class. I entered his room to bring back breakfast plates he snuck upstairs.

"Dad, are you okay?"

I nodded I was fine.

Horowitz called back just as I was entering my home office.

"It's Jason." he said.

"Oscar's in Scripps Hospital."

"Oh fuck." said Horowitz.

"He tried to kill himself. He's in a coma. Have someone cover his classes."

I hung up on Horowitz.

I phoned Gerhardt's neighbor and left a quick message to call me. In the bizarre logistics, I was now mindful about Gerhardt's Golden Retriever. To cover for his neighbor, I could take the dog home or board him at one of those pet hotels in San Diego. Jackie was expected back this week. The events of late had turned me into a circus juggler. I had to prepare for evening class. My nerves were frayed. I had no mental concentration. Teaching via Zoom had the convenience of home but each lecture demanded an element of professionalism. I began obsessing that Gerhardt could die during my class.

Horowitz also had to manage the crisis. He would be forced to alert the divisional dean of Gerhardt's hospitalization. Of course, Horowitz would be discreet in communicating Gerhardt's health to a few, select faculty. Horowitz would have to find a professor who could cover his classes. I wondered if Horowitz was worried about the remote possibility of litigation or reprisals from Gerhardt's family once they discerned Horowitz's role in the sequence of events. An aggressive lawyer might be able to pin Jason Horowitz on charges of hazing and employment intimidation. Undoubtedly, Horowitz would meet with campus counsel in the days ahead.

I found myself in prayer late afternoon. One of the central Jewish *Teffilas* for those who are ill is the *Mi Sheberach*. The name was taken from its first two Hebrew words. With a holistic embrace of human-kind, the Hebrew words ask for a physical cure as well as spiritual healing. Traditionally, the *Mi Sheberach* is said inside a synagogue when the Torah is read. Over recent decades, the *Mi Sheberach* has migrated to secular locales. Chaplains, doctors, social workers, family and friends have been given liberty to say the *Mi Sheberach*. The person who is ill need not be of the Jewish faith. The ritual, for me, was more about devotion than implementing an invisible intervention. More to the point, Gerhardt was born Protestant and rarely attended church. In prayer, I felt connected to Oscar Gerhardt.

Gerhardt's first major publication was in 1987, the year that famed Jewish author and Holocaust survivor Primo Levi died. Gerhardt's book was about the early poets of the Holocaust. Gerhardt ultimately moved to other literary interests. He liked British fiction intensely. There were a few years when Gerhardt focused on Levi. Levi suffered Auschwitz and wrote extensively about his ordeals employing majestic optimism about life's purpose. This was the core to Levi's phenomenal life. To Gerhardt and to the world, Levi's death would remain an unsolved riddle. Primo Levi was sixty-seven when he died after a fall from the stairwell of his third-floor apartment in Turin, Italy. Media reported that Levi had committed suicide. Yet Levi's friends and readers denied that account. He left no note. It was known that Levi battled depression. I recalled Gerhardt talking about Levi's melancholy.

There was no equivalence between Levi and Gerhardt. I linked them nonetheless. Their respective profiles do not match, but there were long battles of sorrow. I did not anticipate Gerhardt's sorrow would be this destructive. My impression from the doctors at Scripps Hospital was that his chances were not good.

Gerhardt revered Levi for tenacity and fighting to live a longer life despite the Holocaust. Gerhardt could only imagine the horrors of a Nazi concentration camp. I say this with awareness that Gerhardt had ridiculed Art Spiegelman's graphic novel investigation of the Holocaust. There was a noble side to Gerhardt and a spiritual dimension too which offset in my mind his scandal. There was ample reason to live despite the humiliations.

Relaying this to Jackie Gerhardt would be futile. There was so much I would like to say to her in the questionable timing of her Ohio trip. I was wrong to judge Gerhardt's wife but I felt that she had a role to play in this disaster. It occurred to me that I was projecting myself onto Gerhardt. We moved through life reasonably and coincidentally as brothers. I was like his older sibling. I could have done more to protect him. My inability to prevent his hospitalization burned me like a Satanic rotisserie.

CHAPTER TWENTY-ONE

I received Yunmei's text with a half-moon emoji asking if we could Facetime 7:30pm Eastern Standard Time. I replied that would be okay for twenty minutes. I required prep time for my evening lecture which included a quiet rest period. I had switched the order of film titles so I could cover Paweł Pawlikowski's 2015 Oscar winning *Ida* from Poland. There were powerful aspects of harsh realism within *Ida* that were reminiscent of early Roman Polanski which was in synch with my clinical mood. The black and white sensibility of this highly distilled, bleak period drama made *Ida* painfully authentic and one of my favorite movies from the last dozen years. Ida, orphaned as a child and about to take vows as a nun, must meet her aunt who was a Communist state prosecutor and last remaining relative. Her atheistic, free-thinking aunt was directed by the church to inform Ida – now called Anna – that her Polish parents were Jewish. The two very mismatched women take to the road to discover their family trauma caused by the Nazi occupation. Ida bonds with her bluntly honest aunt only to be shocked by her aunt's unexpected suicide.

Yunmei had not seen this film although I mentioned *Ida* to her a year ago. Knowing that Yunmei was combating her maniacal Communist aunt from Shanghai added an ironic layer to the film tonight. Why Yunmei requested a video call escaped me. No previous phone conversation with her was on Facetime or Skype.

I ordered pizza delivery for Barry which freed me to go directly from Yunmei to my film class. I also shaved late afternoon to look presentable for class.

Yunmei had initiated the video call on the dot and I took my iPad to the patio.

"Hi Professor Klein. Thank you for making time tonight."

"Hi Yunmei. Nice to see you."

She had on a red blouse and a dark blue cloth mask was draped around her neck like a tight scarf. Her long hair was tied back. It looked like Yunmei was inside the small YMCA guest room.

"I'm getting help from the Associate Dean of Students."

"Oh, that's good news."

"Columbia will notify the Chinese Consulate that my graduate student status is secure and my award scholarship will take me to my master's degree. Online classes will not jeopardize my student visa."

She got out of her chair and went to her door. It wasn't closed firmly and began to open with someone on the other side.

"That's creepy. A crazy lady got the wrong room." she said.

"Lock your door."

"Yes. Yes. What film do you teach tonight?

"Pawlikowski's *Ida*."

"I remember you liked it very much. About Nazis and Catholics in Eastern Europe?"

"Yes."

"It's on my list."

"The story confronts Polish anti-Semitism and cultural self-abnegation."

"Ida is a young nun, yes?"

"She becomes a nun, yes. Her birth name was Ida, but she calls herself Anna. Did you hear from your parents?"

"I did. They think I am twelve years old. Maybe I should become a nun? Maybe I should move to Poland?"

"Is your father in the hospital?"

"Not anymore. He seems better."

"What happened with your aunt over the phone?"

Yunmei's eyes darkened. Her mouth tightened. Her expression was not sullen but there was anger under the surface. I was uncomfortable with the intimacy of seeing her inside her YMCA room. I had set my iPad timer so I could transition to class.

"My mother's sister, Min, is a witch. Isn't that the word?"

"It's a word for somebody you don't like."

"Is a witch worse than a bitch?"

"Both words are bad. She's trying to help your family."

"She's a witch and I hope she flies away on her broom." said Yunmei.

"Your aunt will go back to China as long as you avoid her. Keep your mind on your studies."

"I didn't sleep at the YMCA last night. I had a night adventure."

"A night adventure?"

"I slept with an older grad student."

She moved a few inches away from her computer and was fixing the band which held her hair back. Her eyes were downcast and there were loud sounds outside her room coming from the YMCA corridor.

"Please let's not discuss personal relations."

"He's studying at Union Theological Seminary."

"Yunmei…" I stammered.

"Which is affiliated with Columbia. He has Asperger's and is a little fat with red hair. Cute like a pumpkin. Mr. Halloween. He said he's forty years old and wanted to return to college."

"How nice…"

"His name's Walter Garland. A nice name for a minister. He talks about Reinhold Niebuhr all the time. He is thoughtful, deep, sad. Walter bought me a lobster dinner."

Yunmei was aware of my discomfit, but continued.

"We met while testing for COVID last week. Want to see his photo?"

"No, that's okay."

"I told Walter that I had spray painted one of the Consulate cars early Sunday morning and he was intolerant of any political protests. He says it is a matter of moral good versus adolescent drama."

"Yunmei, listen to me. Walter is right. Stop your war with Chinese authorities. You're risking everything for impulses that you can control.

Your graduate degree and your parents' safety are more important than righteous rage."

She nodded in acknowledging my words but perhaps not embracing them.

"You need to avail yourself of Columbia's psychological counseling services."

"There is a long wait, Professor Klein."

"How long?"

"Three weeks."

"Go back and say it's an emergency."

"It's not an emergency." "It is. You're running from you family. This is exasperating."

"What does that mean?"

"Yunmei, I worry about your well-being. You have the Chinese authorities closing in on you. COVID is out of control. One of my close colleagues is in the hospital because of a prescription overdose. I have to teach two hundred students in a few minutes. My mind is in a thousand places right now. Get counseling now." We just stared at each other on screen.

"We should end Facetime."

"Just five more minutes." She bit her lip.

"Why don't you like me anymore?"

"I like you, Yunmei. You've so much talent."

"Facetime was a mistake. I'm sorry, Professor Klein. I bother you. I don't have Coronavirus. Min flies to Shanghai tomorrow. She will not find me. I hope your friend gets out of the hospital soon."

Yunmei ended the call. I was left with nausea. Was I enabling her? Since her aunt was unable to find Yunmei, Yunmei was free to transgress again. What were the chances that she were to get arrested for vandalism or violence against the Chinese Consulate?

I had forty minutes before my class. I phoned North Shore Hospital to see if there were updates on Benny's condition, but the operator placed me on a rotary directory that kept returning to the main menu. The pizza arrived early and Barry met the delivery's contactless transaction. There was a text from Lamont fishing for news on Gerhardt.

There was also a text from Jason Horowitz asking if he could go to the hospital tonight, as if I could grant him final permission.

I poured a glass of merlot and reviewed my lecture notes. There was too much historical information for class. Tonight wouldn't become a routine lecture because of my preoccupation with Gerhardt. It was reassuring that I could anchor my reservoir of emotion into an analysis of *Ida*. I made the Polish film very personal and appropriated the story. Still, my anxiety was rising. I was dreading Gerhardt's death. I was suffering premonitions that a stronger will could resist. How I wished the wine would take away the edge. No matter how the lecture panned out, I would then drive after class to Scripps Hospital and talk to Gerhardt's medical team.

I went to my laptop, preset several film clips on YouTube, collected my lecture notes, muted my phone, and logged into my Zoom class several minutes before our start. I played a Stan Getz track as lead-in music while my cam was turned off. At 6pm, I greeted the class and asked if students could please set their cameras on to participate. Few would do so, maybe ten percent of the enrollment. I summarized the film studies for the week along with the order of tonight's content. I said that we were switching the order of movies and next week we would watch *The Lives of Others* (*Das Leben der Anderen*) – a 2006 German drama set in 1984, from Florian Henckel von Donnersmarck about the spying of East Berlin citizens by the brutal secret police, the Stasi.

"Tonight we will focus on *Ida*, set twenty years before *The Lives of Others*. These two period films are notable regarding the changing landscape of East Europe's Iron Curtain and the paradoxical rites of individual freedom seen against oppressive regimes and institutions. In 1960s Poland, Anna, a novice nun, was told by her convent that before she took her vows she should see her only living relation, her aunt Wanda Gruz. Anna traveled to visit Wanda, a libertine, sexually promiscuous judge who told Anna that her real identity is Jewess Ida Lebenstein. Ida's parents were killed in World War II. Ida was raised by nuns. Ida's aunt, we learn, was a Communist resistance fighter against the Nazis, and transformed into a renowned state prosecutor

'Red Wanda' with a penchant for sentencing anti-Soviet targets to the fullest extent of the law. This characterization of Wanda, I should highlight, offended several Jewish groups for sketching a stereotype about Polish Jews as collaborators with Communist authorities. Ida's aunt tried to persuade her to sample some sins and pleasures before making her commitment to Christ and the church. Much of the story is a road movie. On their way to their hotel, Wanda picked up a hitchhiker, hoping Ida would be interested in him. A little later, Ida wanted to visit her parents' graves. Her aunt said their graves could be anywhere or perhaps they were not even buried. Ida's aunt questioned her: how would Ida feel if she went to where her parents' remains are and yet sensed that God was absent? Wanda wounded Ida with an unexpected shock as you'll see when you watch the film. And a little later, Ida, wearing her aunt's evening gown and stilettos, did experience sensual pleasures finally sleeping with the hitchhiker. Still, Ida put on her convent habit and returned to the church by story's end. Did she reclaim her soul?"

CHAPTER TWENTY-TWO

I drove to Scripps Hospital with the radio on the nightly news. Any public news would be a welcomed distraction. I thought I would have heard back from Gerhardt's wife by this evening. She didn't call. Was this her way of coping with disaster? Was she paralyzed? I knew Gerhardt had other friends in town, but who would be informing them about Gerhardt's crisis? I wondered if I would be running into Jason Horowitz in the hospital waiting room. Would Gerhardt's brother fly in from Dallas? Did Jackie phone him?

I sensed that Oscar Gerhardt was fighting to stay alive. That was clearly my hope. When I met the nursing staff I was told that there were new concerns. The attending physician clarified that Oscar Gerhardt's liver was failing due to the overdose. Defects in his clotting was an additional worry. The hospital asked me to phone for updates rather than visit due to COVID precautions. I was his only visitor since the ambulance's arrival.

I imagined Oscar's gravelly voice saying that life overwhelmed him with indignities. His voice was in my ear saying, now more than ever, clear his good name, reputation, and his legacy. His voice declared that he wanted seven more good teaching years before retirement. Suicide was a miscalculation. I imagined Oscar, after benefitting from a medical miracle, preparing a self-serving essay for The Chronicle of Higher Education on the loss of academic freedom during the rise of the MeToo movement. I imagined him, in tux and boutonniere, at his daughter's wedding. These thoughts were unreal but comforting. And yes, I imagined Oscar voiceless and in a waking near death state – a clear blue silence.

I sat motionless inside my car in the hospital garage. The face mask was pulling on the ridge of my ears. The weight of anxiety held me. Oscar Gerhardt planned to take his life and his soul might not be around to witness the success of his intention. How long had he contemplated suicide? Had he concocted this plan a year in advance, the consequences still remained perverse. Had he believed surrendering life at age sixty avoided the physical and mental hardships at eighty?

Driving home there were few cars out. At one of the longer traffic lights, I violated the red light with an illegal right turn. My mind was not on the rules of the road. I was driving faster than usual. Thoughts drifted to Ariel. Was I in her thoughts? We once communicated that way.

When I arrived home I heard barking dogs. There was a text from Jackie Gerhardt upset about her father's situation in Akron. She fired the first caregiver and was waiting for an agency to send a replacement. Jackie would now fly back to California on Friday. She was in despair about Oscar. Scripps Hospital was giving her updates.

I then got a call from Celeste while closing the garage door.

"Hi Celeste. You're up late."

"Yes, 11:30pm."

"What's going on?"

"My itinerary shifted. I'm flying to L.A. this Wednesday – a week earlier. I thought I could drive down to San Diego Saturday morning."

"This Saturday."

"Yes. Is that a problem?"

"No. That's great."

"I promise that I won't talk about Tony."

"You can talk about anything."

"How are you?"

"Not well. I just came back from the hospital. A college friend is in a coma."

"Oh God, I'm so sorry."

"It was a suicide attempt."

Celeste was silenced. I didn't wish to elaborate.

"How can I help?" she said.

"It's good to hear your voice. There's nothing to be done. Really. Pray. His wife is in Ohio with a crisis facing her father."

"Is he a close friend?"

"Yeah. He is."

"Did you find him at home?"

"Good guess."

Celeste was empathic.

"Should I skip San Diego?"

"Don't. It would be nice to connect."

"I lost a friend to suicide nine years ago. A fantastic ceramic artist. Her therapist was inept. Her lover was cruel. She isolated herself in her pain."

"It's impossible to take in." I mumbled.

"There are always telltale signs."

"Yeah."

"COVID had caused a spike in suicides."

"Maybe death is a grand release in such cases."

"When I was in high school I thought of killing myself. I hated my friends. I thought that I was bipolar and a freak."

I had recalled in our relationship times when Celeste was suffering depression. Her vulnerability was like phases of the moon.

"The virus has pierced everyone's spirit. Our friends aren't safe to see. We can't touch anything. We build bubbles. Every week the blasé death toll surpasses the week before. Fucking conspiracy theories. Trump will kill us all if he gets a second term."

We agreed to talk Saturday morning for specifics about her drive to San Diego from Los Angeles. I wanted to be in her company, feel her affection.

"I hope your friend pulls through."

"Thanks."

"Sleep well tonight." she said.

Entering the house I remembered to transpose the Zoom recorded lecture to Media Gallery in the Canvas software so asynchronous students could watch class. I checked in with Barry who was playing a video game. I sent a text to Colby. There was a missed call and voicemail from Max Edelmann.

My phone rang a few minutes later. It was Lamont. I took the call and anticipated Lamont having news about Gerhardt. But I was wrong.

"I've a scandal that will entertain you."

"Not tonight."

"Got a girlfriend over?"

"No."

"Well, I'll make it short. You know I'm on the promotions and tenure committee."

"Yeah I know. It's all confidential."

"I'll speak algebra. A full professor in our division was nailed for extensive plagiarism found in his first publication twenty years ago."

I was non-responsive.

"You *know* this guy, Jonathan. He pissed off a lot of folks. Dickensian irony. More precisely, pages out of a David Lodge novel."

"Did he admit to the charges?"

"Not yet. He hasn't been formally charged. He used unattributed content from a deceased Japanese scholar, translated into English. About forty pages that are stunningly correlated. The stolen material was the heart of his long article."

"Truly horrible."

"And one of his graduate students made the discovery."

"Why are you telling me?"

"Because he's in your department."

"I need to go and check in with my son."

"I'll let you go. But let me give one more clue."

Again, I was non-responsive.

"His initials are . . . JH. As in Jason Horowitz."

"Skip. I didn't hear any of this. I'm hanging up."

CHAPTER TWENTY-THREE

Tuesday morning, October 6th, took on extraordinary complications. Throughout the news cycle were video clips of the world's most famous COVID patient – Donald J. Trump, looking high on steroids and other medications – returning to the White House lawn from a Marine One helicopter and climbing the balcony stairs to remove his black face mask. The obese, reddened president was gasping for breath while holding a Mussolini pose for an army of cameras. Maskless, Trump then instructed one photographer to stand inches behind him for a reverse angle. Everything darkly poetic about the plague was on exhibit during this ironic photo op. Alien galaxies watching would assume our imbecilic culture was doomed. There were now over two hundred thousand American deaths from Coronavirus. But one American, who only paid seven hundred and fifty dollars in federal taxes while living cost-free at 1600 Pennsylvania Avenue, received a privileged, experimental treatment not approved for the public. His COVID medical fees and hospital transport were over one hundred thousand dollars paid for by the American taxpayer.

I was rested to greet an easier day. I listened to Max Edelmann's garbled, emotive phone message after reading the iPhone transcription which was comedic due to his New York accent.

"I can hire someone to *curdle* you . . ."

And the other classic line.

"Someone could break both of your *fracking eggs* . . ."

I decided not to phone him back but I did compose a very lengthy text which was an example of my irrational death wish.

"Max, I got your phone message. My prayers go to your father. I worry in good conscience about flying Cassandra to NY lest the cat come down with COVID. The last two days she was sneezing & coughing up fur balls. Honest to God, I've no problem paying ATW (Animal Transportation Worldwide) $7000 to escort her – not including gratuities to drivers, to the pilot, & the certifying veterinarian. But shipping a geriatric cat cross country during a heat wave & a pandemic makes you and me villains. Do you really want her to die?"

Max Edelmann texted back immediately saying, "I'm coming to your front door before the end of the week, you cocksucker. You'll wish you were never born."

With this text and his voicemail last night, I believed I had enough to go to the police in garnering some protection.

Gerhardt's neighbor Phoebe, who was caring for the Gerhardt dog Zorro, phoned. She asked how Oscar was doing. Phoebe were driving to Orange County in a few hours and asked if I could pick up the Gerhardt dog. She said there was no pet boarding facility to take Zorro without veterinary health records. Phoebe promised me that Zorro was the sweetest dog she had ever housed.

"I don't know if I can, Phoebe. My son is afraid of large dogs."

"Zorro's not a dog. He's a Golden Retriever. He won't harm a fly."

"I'll talk to my son. How long are you gone?"

"I'll be home in four days and happy to have Zorro back."

I agreed to pick up the Golden Retriever. Phoebe had dog food, dog bed, dog treats, and non-allergic dog shampoo. After our phone call I recalled a recurring dream involving Traci, Oscar and his wife Jackie. The four of us in a motorboat. Everyone was berating me for throwing life vests overboard. The vessel had trouble with large wakes. One wave hit our craft with a punishing perpendicular blow. We all fell into the harbor.

When I ran into Barry, he was loading the clothes washer and said we were out of detergent. I suggested he run tap water into the Tide jug and add dishwasher detergent into the mix. He gave me a look. I wasn't in the mood to run to the store for one item but he said he also needed deodorant. That made no sense to me since Barry doesn't go anywhere, even on weekends.

My urgency was to contact a friend Fred Woodruff – from karate school twenty years ago – now a San Diego police lieutenant and a good Samaritan. There really was a threat of violence in my life. Max Edelmann was on my legal yellow pad. His name seen as large block letters in the manner of my first grade penmanship. Fred was already monitoring Ariel's whereabouts during her phantom escapades from home in past months when she was a minor. Now I would be asking Fred a second favor.

Max's menace on face value felt improbable. How could he abandon New York for a day or two while his father battles COVID in the ICU? Why would he elevate a cat into an interstate kidnapping? Why did he have this immense animosity towards me? Was this *Sturm und Drang* Max's psychotic acting out? Did Benny tell his son that I was in the will?

If only I could get Benny on the phone, this dispute with some diplomacy could dissipate. Should Benny lose his life to COVID, Max would proceed in all of his destructive energies. Maybe the wisest action would be to convince Max in writing that I willingly forfeit anything assigned in the will, ensuring that he would be the sole beneficiary. I never wanted a penny of Benny's estate, particularly with this existential provocation. Any largesse from Benny would be cursed forever.

Did Benny have great wealth? That was the overpowering legend I knew. Were there hidden sources to his wealth? Did Benny own points in a high-profile casino? Did he have real estate in Nevada, New York and Florida? Would his assets be problematic in probate? How many names were denoted in his written will? In the news a year ago, Chanel designer Karl Lagerfeld had designated his cat Choupette an inheritance capturing most of his $195 million estate. Would Cassandra be as lucky?

Our American *zeitgeist* was turning dark, fed on controversial

Trump years and global illness. The Trump Presidency had inverted America's role, once the free world's leader. Moreover, Trumpian madness gave us a byproduct upsetting academia and driving universities toward overcorrected social justice mania. Responsible media in 2015 became addicted to Trump's daily headline mechanics and the addiction to his White House reality show drilled deep into our marrow. We pinned our hope on the Mueller Report which delivered nothing of resolve. Under this Administration we separated young children from their refugee parents along our southern border. We kept the children and toddlers in cages. America could not find many of the parents to reunify the families.

Progressive critics had bristled, to say the least, at the notion that Trump was only a fatter and more racist version of cinema's Gordon Gekko. It was in Oliver Stone's *Wall Street* where we witnessed Gekko's "greed is good" motto, branding the era of Ronald Reagan. Were the 1980s more humane than the age of Trump? The comparison was a challenge. Reagan's administration failed in confronting HIV, crack, and the murder rate in American cities. These horrors targeted communities outside of Reagan's Shiny City on a Hill. Trump's damage to democracy could be divided by one third racism, one third nativism, and one third fascism. We privatized our prisons to profitable companies. Our police employed army weapons and even army tanks. According to many pundits on the left, we still live and die on our American plantation, masters and slaves.

Far right websites had promoted a bloody civil war during our summer and fall. Portland and Seattle had previewed the look of this riotous nightmare protesting police racism. QAnon had alleged that Satanic pedophiles were gunning for Trump. The crazies on the far right imagine a spectacular revolution to purify the planet. The revolt will spawn concentration camps for errant journalists and politicians. For years Trump was cast as the savior in the eyes of QAnon followers. We slipped tragically, one foot into Philip Roth's *The Plot Against America*, and the other foot, into Albert Camus' *The Plague*.

I decided to drive to Phoebe's early afternoon. I had lied about Barry fearing large dogs. It was a reflexive fib to avoid obligation. I was ready to help the Gerhardt family. Phoebe thanked me warmly. She expressed optimism about Oscar's recovery despite the severity of his coma. I tried to share her optimism. Phoebe expressed over the phone that she was a creature of strong faith.

I had met Gerhardt's large reddish dog many times before. I just didn't recall him calling the Golden Retriever Zorro. I thought he called his dog Red. I liked the name Red. I wanted to call him Red. Zorro sounded like a Tinder username or the handle Secret Service gave to a member of the President's extended family.

In my literal mind there were only two masked Zorros in contemporary culture: early TV's Guy Williams (né Armando Joseph Catalano) who went on to play the father in *Lost In Space* taking his American family to colonize Alpha Centauri; and Spain's rakish film star Antonio Banderas, in the 1998 blockbuster *The Mask of Zorro* who went on to play the dashing father in *Spy Kids* among numerous other hit films. Was Gerhardt's family thinking Guy Williams or Antonio Banderas? The fictional character was modeled on Mexican folktales of a noble thief who battled the rich on behalf of the poor and the indigenous. Zorro was invented by author Johnston McCulley in 1919. Douglas Fairbanks played the role in 1920 and Tyrone Power in 1940. The name means the fox in Spanish.

Which Zorro was projected onto the Gerhardt dog?

Phoebe helped load the dog's accessories into my car. Zorro was mellow, curious, and fond of licking anything which moved slowly. He went into the back seat with a little lift from me. I was certain he weighed around eighty pounds. Phoebe had a tender manner in talking to the dog. "This was a good deed for the day" said Phoebe. She had a hidden dog treat in her jeans' pocket. Before we closed the car door, Phoebe slipped Zorro the biscuit and cycled to her positive outlook.

"Jonathan, I'm a very religious person. We have to trust God."

"Thanks, Phoebe."

"I hope you can believe this too."

"Yes."

"God tests us. We test God."

"Yes, we do."

"This must be very hard on Jackie and their daughter."

"Yes."

"This must be very hard on you."

"Yes."

"God loves us." she said. "Heaven exists."

I got into the car and drove away. Zorro blocked my sightlines as I glanced into the rearview mirror. He looked handsome, wise, and self-possessed. He looked happy. I began talking to Zorro while driving, something I had picked up driving Cassandra from Benny's Atria. This seemed normal, not peculiar. I told Zorro what Phoebe told me. It occurred to me that people around the world talk to their animals at great length and this might be the key to our tenuous survival.

In my mental maelstrom, the 1989 French horror film *Baxter* directed by Jérôme Boivin materialized. Unlike talking dogs on television and in films, sardonic Baxter was not a charmer. He is a killer Bull Terrier who narrated his Dostoevsky tale searching for a well-appointed pet keeper. TV Guide panned the film calling it bleak, vile, nihilistic and a graphic depiction of all that can go sour between a diabolic dog and various human owners. Certainly, Zorro would be the yang to Baxter's yin as we headed home.

CHAPTER TWENTY-FOUR

A ray of sunshine pierced the heavy gray clouds. Oscar Gerhardt's status had changed incrementally as it was noted that his eyes were blinking earlier this morning, according to the phone call from Scripps. This was not a miracle but hearing the news lifted my spirits. The doctors had underscored that spontaneous blinking to medical stimuli was a positive sign that the reticular system was functioning and wakefulness was present. I was cautioned that while wakefulness was necessary for consciousness, wakefulness alone was inadequate for desired consciousness. Gerhardt and his immediate world were separated by degrees of wakefulness.

The research on overdose-induced comas I did online indicated that cases vary greatly and recovery patterns were not always plain to see. Many patients resuscitated after drug overdose, trauma or anoxic injury transition into a chronic vegetative state. The longer the coma, the less likely a recovery.

If there were afterlife states, would patients in a coma hold a glimpse? Would coma patients be able to choose life on earth or journey to an afterworld? Would Gerhardt choose an option? Was the question similar to playing blackjack and drawing a second card?

These concerns were rattling me as I walked the dog around my neighborhood. Zorro was fine on the leash. He didn't pull. I found him responding to vocal commands and radiating contentment. His stride had a rhythmic sashay. Perhaps this was the beginning of hip dysplasia? A whitish rabbit with black nose and black ears materialized near the hedges. Zorro noticed the rabbit and jerked the lead. I wondered what omen a white rabbit presented. This non-native critter was purchased at a pet store and found her way to our suburbia.

Zorro looked back at me for assurances as we walked. I respected Zorro for this flirtatious eye contact. Many dogs share their joy to enter parks and circle neighborhoods. Towards the end of our stroll, Zorro made a deposit on a meticulously maintained lawn that surrounded a sleek house framed by wood and stucco. In my pocket were pleasantly scented poop bags with a blue paw print pattern. Phoebe had instructed me how to pry the bag open – wet one's fingers with a swipe of the tongue and pinch the sealed bag open.

I prepared dinner for Barry and me after feeding Zorro and took Fred Woodruff's call. Fred read my email which had screenshots of Max Edelmann's text and iPhone transcription of Max's voice messages. Fred asked me a volley of questions and took down information about his profile in Larchmont, New York. Fred would run a trace on Max's background. Fred referenced that Congress had passed twenty-five years ago an anti-stalking law. It was a federal felony to cross state lines to stalk or harass if the conduct causes fear of bodily injury or death to the stalking victim. This was part of the Violence Against Women Act. He advised me to take precautions – keeping doors and windows locked, checking the car before driving it, avoid going out in the evening, and be guarded in public spaces and parking areas. The Lieutenant counseled me to let Barry know about the threat so that nothing would catch us by surprise.

After washing the dishes, I received a phone call via my iPad. It was Yunmei.

"Hello Professor."

"Hi Yunmei."

"How is your friend in the hospital?"

"Still in a coma but there is some eye movement."

"Oh my God…I am so sorry."

"Thank you."

"This is a difficult time for you."

"Yes."

"I want to tell you good news." she said with emotion.

"Please do."

"My aunt went back to Shanghai."

"Wonderful."

"She couldn't find where I was staying and she got sick in the city."

"And your parents?"

"Better. The Chinese authorities let my mother go home. I get emails from her again. She wants me to finish my masters at Columbia in eighteen months."

"That's workable, Yunmei."

"Yes. And she wants me to cancel my Vimeo, TikTok, YouTube accounts. No more videos. No more political blogs. It will destroy our family, she said."

"Well, she is meeting you in the middle. That's an improvement."

"Yes, if I can trust what she is saying."

"How is the YMCA?"

"It is okay. The room is super tiny. They let you use the indoor swimming pool despite COVID. I'm close to Central Park. Maybe I can find something better now that Min has returned to China. A roommate is cheaper than living at the Y."

"Things seem better."

"I guess so. I streamed *Ida* today. It's good. The film felt like Ingmar Bergman. So contained and intimate. It seemed that the church was complicit, no better than the state, and yet the church attempted to open both doors for Ida. The film reminded me of De Sica's *Two Women – La ciociara –* from 1960."

Yunmei stopped her train of thought and said a word or two in Mandarin which escaped me. Then a moment of silence.

"I have to tell you something about our Facetime call yesterday."

Another silence.

"Professor, I didn't tell the truth yesterday. I lied to you. I am so sorry. I am acting strange."

"You don't have to apologize."

"I do. I want to fix this."

"Okay."

"Thank you. Ask me." she said.

"What was the lie?"

"Can you guess it?"

"No."

"The lie was about Walter Garland."

"And?"

"I didn't spend the night with him. I hardly know him."

"Is he the divinity graduate student?"

"Yes."

"But you like him?"

"Not really. He's jerk."

"Does he like you?"

"Yes."

"Why did you make this up?"

"I wanted to see how you would react. How you would judge me."

"I didn't judge you."

"I thought you did."

"I didn't."

"And you weren't jealous?"

"No."

"That's why I want you to know that I made this up."

"I understand."

"I am not a person who lies."

"Yunmei, I see you as a truthful person."

"Thank you, Professor Klein. I want you to know that everything else I have told you is true. I always tell true things."

"Good."

"When will you come back to New York?"

"Not for a long time."

"You should come next month, Professor."

"Let's see what happens with the contagion."

Yunmei hung up having expressed relief that she had set, in her own words, an ethical correction. I was puzzled by her behavior, but her voice struck me as truthful. Maybe she did sleep with this divinity student Walter Garland. Maybe casual sexual encounters in New York were part of her human drive. I could not intuit what was at root in this exchange.

Barry met me in the kitchen with papers.

"I need your signature for a syllabus contract with the college. Sociology. It's the one course not taught by my high school."

"Is it AP?"

"Yes."

"Shouldn't I read the contract before signing?"

"Why? You've seen a thousand of these."

"Well, did you read the syllabus?"

"Yeah."

"And?"

"It's a syllabus."

I flipped through the pages and signed it.

"Thanks." Barry said.

This would have been a good moment to have told Barry about Max Edelmann's stalking. Was it embarrassment that held me back? I decided to tell him tomorrow. The image of the white rabbit stayed in my mind. I Googled symbolism + white rabbit. According to a shaman website with a profile photo resembling Wanda Sykes, a white rabbit represents the hollow. The hollow signifies emptiness and opportunity to fill life anew. If I further my spirituality, I have the support of this Wanda Sykes shaman. She would like my credit card number. If I delve into the vortex, I will be commended by this beautiful Wandy Sykes.

"Do not fear the evolution you are making dear one. The white rabbit reminds you to step forward through your phobias, as you start to feel the mystical, metaphysical and supernatural aspects even more, now or in the coming times."

CHAPTER TWENTY-FIVE

Just before going to sleep, came a call from Jackie Gerhardt.

"Sorry to call so late. I was trying to reach you earlier but misplaced your number."

"That's okay, Jackie."

"Phoebe gave it to me."

"She asked that I watch your dog." I said.

"Yes, you are *an angel*. The hospital said that Oscar's eyes have movement. That he may have entered into a recovery phase."

"That's what I heard too."

"Our family owes you so much, Jonathan."

"Oscar would do the same for me."

"I called to confirm that I'll be in San Diego late Saturday afternoon. My father had coverage issues and his health problem just slammed us. My whole family is falling apart. I can't believe the last few days. Can you manage with Zorro?"

"Zorro's no problem, Jackie."

"That's really great. Just remember no table scraps of any kind or he'll have the runs. Just the food that Phoebe gave you."

"Of course."

"And in case he does any counter surfing or swipes food you forget to put away, take him to the vet immediately. Diarrhea is more serious with his tricky GI tract. Goldens are the most delicate large dogs."

"Who's your vet?"

"Beach Veterinary on Prospect. I'll text you address and phone FYI."

"How's your daughter handling this?"

"Penelope's okay all in all. We both know that Oscar's going to make it." she said distinctly.

I thought that we concluded the requisite transactions and waited for the call to end. But Jackie was clearing her throat and we lapsed into a silence.

"He was born with strong will power." I said. "We're all praying that he'll pull through."

"Do you know this Brenda girl?" she asked.

"Hardly. She was in one of my seminars."

"Well, let her know the goddamn damage she caused. And if he dies, she's responsible."

Jackie got off the phone. I walked by Barry's room and bid him a good night. Barry was in a humor and asked me which was a greater invention in our lifetime: condoms, superglue, or Velcro? What was the connection to the choices? A close fit? Zorro was in my office making sounds between operatic warmups and Chewbacca. I went to check. The door was closed. Zorro must know that I was never the dog whisperer. Still, Zorro didn't like being left alone all night. Notably, the beautiful dog had a case of flatulence. One could hear his exhaust or one could detect with olfactory certainty.

He had knocked over things from my desk and found the TV remote to play with on the coffee table. Nothing was destroyed. I sensed there was risk leaving him alone in this room. With the office door open, he hurried down the corridor towards our bedrooms. Perhaps he had sensed where the house alpha was going to bed down? I relented and allowed Zorro to sleep in my bedroom. Zorro found an area shag rug by the bay window. This was his spot. He circled and collapsed into a perfect sleeping posture.

It was at this moment that I had visualized Traci inside our home. This didn't disturb me. This was the mercy of memory. A canine served as the medium to a ghostly presence. Traci, in a silk white house robe, turning towards the left. Turning towards the right. Attending to her long hair with one hand like an actor inside a dressing room. Toying with a thin gold necklace, her face tilted to extend the length of her swan neck. Her bare feet pointing forward like a Degas ballerina. I imagined this and nothing more.

I looked at the framed photo of Traci on my desk. She had on a tennis hat and the shot was taken at Casa Del Zorro Desert Resort in Borrego Springs. Traci looked ten years younger than her age, radiant, beautiful, and happy. I know in my heart that she had solace in most things and always included me in her solace.

When I stirred the next morning, I was not alone in bed. My body was spooning with Zorro. He had more duvet than me. In *Moby Dick*, Ishmael accepted the innkeeper's proposal to share the one vacant bed with Queequeg, a tattooed Polynesian harpooner who wanted to sell an embalmed South Seas human head. Like Melville's Ismael, I had survived the night in a large bed with a creature so strange. Barry walked into the bedroom and saw the two of us in bed.

"The fucking WiFi's out and my class began fifteen minutes ago."

I phoned the cable company. The dog did not move an inch. While I was on hold with Spectrum, I asked myself what an embalmed head would cost today adjusted for inflation.

"Barry," I shouted, " this could take a half hour. Log into Zoom with your phone."

"Cell service sucks in my room."

While waiting for Spectrum, Lamont phoned. I let Lamont go to voicemail.

Twenty minutes had passed. I forced myself to be stoic. Finally, the Spectrum agent announced himself with an exotic accent from the other hemisphere.

"There was a temporary outage and a signal would soon return. You are instructed to call back in three hours or Spectrum will call you once service is restored. Please stay on the phone for a three minute survey about how I was able to help you today."

I texted Barry with the news that Specturm has a regional problem which should be fixed in an hour or two. Zorro was ready for his morning walk. We went out not quite dressed for the public. I called back Lamont along the walk.

"How's Gerhardt?" Lamont asked.

"You heard?"

"Yeah." he said with compassion. "How tragic."

"Grim news travels fast."

"You found him?"

"Yes." I replied.

"You're like Marilyn Monroe's psychiatrist."

I accidently dropped the phone.

"Her shrink found her in bed. The first to lay eyes on the corpse."

Zorro pooped steps away from the phone.

"So I heard from a reliable source that Horowitz will skate to safety. Upper administration has his back. He'll get a one paragraph 'advisory letter' in his file from the Associate Chancellor and that will be that. Nothing will leave the review committee. It's a buried issue. The guy's wrapped in Teflon."

"I could give a shit about Horowitz's file."

"Word to the wise, Jonathan. Horowitz's not your friend."

"I didn't think he was." I muttered while bagging the excrement.

"I'm warning you."

"Thanks."

"You're welcome."

"Animals don't worry about death."

"Where did that come from?" Lamont asked.

"I had a mixed chocolate Labrador when I was a kid. Around age eight I had my first bout of thanatophobia, so I tried to emulate the dog. It worked."

"How did you emulate a dog?"

"Well, you start by licking your balls."

"Very funny, Jonathan."

Lamont changed the topic.

"You know, COVID is spiking on our campus but we're seeing the most accurate data."

"You suspect the administration is suppressing numbers?"

"Nothing is far-fetched."

"Maybe our campus isn't considerate to the community beyond our walls? Students can be super-spreaders."

"Yeah, even if we're testing students weekly. We're looking at res life sewage. We should send all the students home for online learning only. The Chancellor's like the mayor in the movie *Jaws*."

Lamont laughed and hung up. Spectrum called back. Our Wi-Fi was working. San Diego Gas and Electric was controlling outages during the wildfires.

I returned Jason Horowitz's call. He picked up.

"How's Gerhardt's condition?"

"A little better. There was some eye movement yesterday."

"Jesus, that's some good news."

He asked me to maintain discretion as any circulating news about Oscar would be harmful to his family and our department. I thought that was farcical in light of Lamont getting rumors. But then Horowitz dropped a bomb with the delicacy of a *maître d'* at Olive Garden.

"Jonathan, the last few weeks I've been in dialogue with the dean on the debilitating campus budget due to COVID. As you know, there's a hiring freeze. Deans have to work their alchemy to survive. Several academic departments are forced to compress and to consolidate. Our sister department Visual Arts had many recent senior retirements. They're not in a good way. So the dean asked me to consider transferring you to Visual Arts to beef up their enrollment numbers with your popular film classes and, by doing so, our department can accommodate a spousal hire who is African American. We've so many white males in Literature while Vis Arts is far more diversified. Clearly, you can teach all the classes you like and as a stop gap measure Vis Arts and Lit will cross-list them for future academic years. You'll draw your TAs from Vis Arts. We have no teaching assistants to spare. The dean said you'll get your above scale promotion more readily in Vis Arts than our own department, so this will be a godsend to you. You'll have the Distinguished Professor title in short order. The dean will also provide you one course release this year as an incentive to migrate. I realize that you have a few close colleagues in Lit but they're scheduled to retire in the next year or so. I know that this week's a terrible time to throw the notion at you."

"Jason..." I was dumbstruck.

"But it's vital to finalize things by October 12th. You can confirm with us by Friday, if that's okay."

"Jason, you must be joking."

"I'm not joking, Jonathan."

"Look. I'm all for enhancing diversity hiring for our department."

"I'm know you are. You've been a strong advocate for equity, diversity and inclusion."

"But you can't take away my tenure in our department."

"No one's removing tenure. You're employed for life by the university."

"My original hire letter assigned me to the Department of Literature."

"The letter was not the contractual document."

"I've documents that are contractual, Jason."

"More to the point, Jonathan. You're still in the Division of Arts and Humanities. Ostensibly you have a choice. In reality what choice have you? Word will get out if your inflexibility prevented an appointment of a person of color."

"Come on, Jason. Put yourself in my position. My decades of service to our department. My pride. You know how I feel."

"I do. Please know the chair of Vis Arts is excited to have you."

A deafening silence.

"And if I say no?"

"No?"

"No."

"No is what a toddler would say. No is not the answer we want to hear today."

CHAPTER TWENTY-SIX

I forced the ludicrous Horowitz phone call out of my consciousness. He was correct technically. I have a choice in the matter. We are not in the United States military. However, Horowitz's tone was militant. He seemed to have a master plan of ridding the department of Gerhardt and me within the school year. I reminded myself that my hardship as presented by the department chair was one hundredth that of Oscar Gerhardt's. Why can't the campus remember the best of Gerhard's published works and career as an educator?

Oscar wrote a superb, underappreciated study in 1990 on the novels of Anthony Burgess. This achievement was dramatically unlike the following decades of Gerhardt's research, teachings and publications as he pivoted to the graphic novel's significance in contemporary culture. Gerhardt had met Burgess several times in England before he passed away in 1993. I believe that he even had heard him lecture at City College of New York in 1972 when Gerhardt was a freshman at Stuyvesant High School. Gerhardt savored Burgess' ability to be playful like a trickster, satirical, unpredictable, esoteric, iconoclastic, restless, vulgar, and fearless with Joycean literary conceits. Burgess, a consummate linguist, was best known for *A Clockwork Orange* published in 1962. According to published interviews and features, Burgess mostly detested the book's celebration and, even more, Stanley Kubrick's controversial and violent film adaptation. If legend were to be believed, Burgess received five hundred dollars for the film rights, but the property bought him amazing subsequent income and publicity for his literary output. Burgess saw himself beyond mere novelist; he was a classical composer, librettist, literary critic, lecturer, expatriate, and a prankster.

Gerhardt's book had tremendous insights into Burgess' four comic novels on the dyspeptic poet Enderby, who composed on a toilet and kept a life of solitude in Brighton, England, supported by investments from his stepmother. This Wednesday afternoon, I decided to reread sections of this critical study and it was very gratifying to reconnect with a side of Gerhardt that had vanished. Immersing myself this way intensified an immutable tie between Gerhardt and me. Certainly, I cherished his more traditional scholarship, his previous formalism, and Gerhardt's early love of post-war and late century British novelists. Gerhardt even allowed himself an indulgence commenting on Anthony Burgess having dared to write a review of his own book, *Inside Mr. Enderby* – originally under the pseudonym Joseph Kell – for the modest *Yorkshire Post*. Upon discovering that Mr. Kell was an alias, *Yorkshire Post* fired Burgess. Gerhardt loved Burgess' prank and loved doubly having the newspaper dump his literary idol.

Gerhardt's precision, authority, analysis, and agility in the Burgess book heralded greater studies to come from Gerhardt, which regrettably hadn't panned out.

I found healing in this rediscovery of Gerhardt's writing today. It was a fitting respite from Horowitz's rapacious phone call and updates from North Shore University Hospital. I was in denial about too many concerns crashing down. My mind repeated the sequence of entering Gerhardt's house, finding him unconscious, waiting for the ambulance, hearing the doctor's report. The venal behavior of Jason Horowitz, directed at Gerhardt and at me, was par for the course at a powerhouse campus unsupportive of the arts. Horowitz knew that it was humiliating and a transgression to push a tenured senior faculty member against the professor's wishes to another academic department. More typically, a professor would make the request to move to a sister department because of some incompatible issue with colleagues or a considerable opportunity in the receiving department. For those in the hard sciences and supporting large costly labs, a transfer can be dear to both departments. Horowitz, had he a soul, would have framed this differently as a voluntary option.

If Gerhardt were not in the hospital, not the target of a sexual harassment charge, he would circulate a petition defending my rights to upper administration. Skip Lamont would not. Further, I would not mobilize any colleague to take up the sword on my behalf. No winners would arise from that action. I decided to keep the news of Horowitz's maneuver from my son, but over breakfast I updated Barry about Benny's unhinged son.

"Just be a bit more alert around the house. Check the windows. Don't answer the door unless you recognize the face. And Max is very short."

"How long does this have to go on?"

"Maybe a week. Maybe a month." I said. "The police know and will help us."

"And this is because of the cat?"

"Yes...and no."

"Pretty weird shit." said Barry.

"Benny Edelmann had helped your grandfather a long time ago."

Barry looked flummoxed. He knew this was a real concern.

"This weekend, an old friend will be visiting."

"Who?"

"Celeste."

"I remember that name."

"You do?"

"From New York?"

"Yes."

"Is she still hot?"

"No one over the age of fifty is hot."

"J.Lo is." he said in a half smile.

"Yeah, I stand corrected."

"What do you think of Jane Fonda?"

"She's over eighty." I said.

"Yep. She is." Barry said.

"Let's not mention Max Edelmann during Celeste's visit. It will spook her."

"Okay."

"Thanks."

"And how long is the dog staying?"

"Until Saturday. He's no trouble. You're not allergic to him?"

"No. Just wondering what animal comes after Zorro."

"A llama."

"No llamas, Dad. They spit from a distance of twenty feet."

"That's a myth. Llamas only spit at tourists visiting Machu Picchu."

Barry left the kitchen with a donut wrapped in a napkin. Donuts were his greatest weakness, his sweet Kryptonite. I went to my office to gather material for my next lecture. Settling into a work period would offset the morning funk. I reflected on Yunmei's *Ida* remarks, impressed that she watched the movie, her tangent to De Sica's *La ciociara*, and perplexed that she admitted to a falsehood. I wondered whether Yunmei watching *Ida* assisted her softening any edges towards her Shanghai aunt. The more I became familiar with Yunmei, the less I could intimate her opaqueness which mixed so strangely with her sincerity.

My phone rang. It was Benny. I didn't think he would be on the line and suspected Max got hold of his father's phone. So I let it go unanswered and there was a voice message. I went to hear it and there was Benny's definitive voice:

"Jonathan, call me back. It's Benny. I'm in a hospital but I can talk."

I was astonished. I called him at once.

"Benny, it's Jonathan."

"I just called you."

"I know." I said.

"I'm in North Shore Hospital. I was on a fucking ventilator. The doctors are awful. I got the damn virus."

"I heard."

"Who told you?"

"Your son Max."

"Maxie called you?"

"Yeah, the other day."

Benny sounded weak and distant. There was a slight echo to the call.

"Well, I'll be here for a week or so. That's what the doctor said. I lost weight. I look like shit. I hate hospitals. Listen Jonathan, you must have done something bad to Maxie. He's really pissed."

"I know Benny."

"So maybe you tell me the truth."

"Sure."

"Don't bullshit me."

"I'm not going to bullshit you."

"No one bullshits me." Benny said.

"Your son called as soon as you were admitted to the hospital. He had an emergency contact sheet. I was on it. He's pissed because of Cassandra."

"So he called you after I left Atria?"

"Max wanted to know why I had your cat and if I had some game going on."

"You have Cassandra?"

This startled me. He was forgetting. Coronavirus had that effect.

"Yes, you wanted me to be her foster home in San Diego. Atria didn't allow pets."

Benny took a few moments to put his memory in place.

"You're in California?"

"That's right."

"Why the fuck would I want you to take the cat to California?"

"I don't know. It had to do something with my father."

"Your father owed me money, Jonathan."

"I know, Benny."

"I gave him more cash than any bank. I liked your father."

"You told me that when I had visited you the other week."

"Did I ask you to take pictures of the cat?"

"Yeah."

"Did you?"

163

"Yes. I sent them to your phone. Look at your texts."

"I got my phone back today."

"That's good, Benny."

"So why did you pick a fight with Maxie?"

"Maybe he wanted to watch the cat?"

"No, no, no. He hates cats."

"What did Max tell you?"

"He said that you're a grifter and a scumbag."

"I'm a college professor, Benny."

"Really? Which college?"

I wanted to flush my phone down the toilet.

"You can't be a grifter if you're a professor. You can be a college scumbag, but I swear to you that I'm not a scumbag."

That made Benny laugh which ignited a chain of coughing.

"Fucking cough. I'm not supposed to talk on the phone long. The cat's okay?"

"Cassandra's fine."

"Keep feeding the cat."

"Of course."

"A fat cat is a happy cat. Cassandra's fat."

"Benny, please do me a favor."

"What?"

"Tell your son I'm not screwing you."

"Okay, Jonathan. I hear you."

"And take me out of your will. You said you put me in your will. He may have read your will."

"Oh, is that it … how did he read my will?"

"I have no idea. Maybe he went through your things at Atria?"

"Maxie wouldn't do that."

"This is getting dangerous. Your son made threats."

"My boy's all bark, no bite."

"He made violent threats."

"You're three thousand miles away."

"Benny, please. Listen to me."

"I'm listening, *boychik.*"

"Revise your will *and let Max know.*"

"Yeah, yeah, yeah. Got to go. The doctor just came in."

Benny hung up.

CHAPTER TWENTY-SEVEN

Celeste left an upbeat, funny phone message announcing her arrival in Los Angeles. She had checked into the Ritz-Carlton, Marina del Rey. She was bumped to business, her flight was half empty, and she loved watching the Korean hit *Parasite* on board.

"Call anytime Jonathan, this is a travel day. Nothing scheduled. Oh, and I tipped the pilot for a quiet flight."

She might connect with her cousin in Long Beach unless her cousin was in deep quarantine state. I imagined her sojourn to California would be better than previous ones when our stars were not quite aligned to her desire. Or to mine. I admitted to myself that I wanted something from her.

The Golden Retriever, agitated and chuffing, paced throughout the house and signalled a growing interest inches from the entrance door. I grabbed his leash and took Zorro out. He had a bout of diarrhea on the front steps. We walked hurriedly into the street where he urinated. In a few minutes he had another explosive loose bowel movement. He began to eat grass, which concerned me about his GI tract. When we circled back to the house, I hosed off the front steps and took paper towels to Zorro's bottom. I asked Barry whether he had noticed if the dog ate anything from the kitchen or his room.

"Dad, it's possible Zorro might have had some Doritos on a plate by my computer. But at least it wasn't the Flamin' Hot Doritos."

"Not good, Barry."

"Yeah, and we're out of Doritos now."

I contacted Beach Veterinary getting a 11:30am appointment today.

I thought anything could happen inside with Zorro, so a room with a hard wood floor might be better than a carpet. I put Zorro in the den. There was a text from Lieutenant Woodruff. He had news on Max Edelmann. I phoned the Lieutenant.

"Jonathan, we had alerted all the rental offices in the area and Enterprise flagged Maxwell Edelmann getting a Nissan Sentra at the airport last night. Luckily, he gave Enterprise his address at Doubletree downtown. An officer was able to reach Edelmann this morning at the hotel. Mr. Edelman was unarmed. To the best of my knowledge, he was escorted back to the airport and was placed on a return flight to Westchester, New York."

"Just like that, Fred?"

"Just like that. Yes. He was warned and told that federal authorities will be alerted. He seemed compliant. He has no previous arrests. He had no firearms."

"So what do you think?" I asked.

"I think you should continue to exercise caution."

"There's still a risk?"

"Yes. We hope that once the police intercedes, the problem dissipates. Nothing is predicable about personal safety. We would have taken him in if he failed to board the plane."

"Thanks, Fred."

"Of course. Stay safe."

Barry came into the kitchen. I told him about Max flying back.

"That's better than having the jerk stalk us."

"Yeah. I'm taking the dog to the vet in an hour."

"Okay."

"No snacks in your room until this dog goes back to Gerhardt's home."

"Yeah, Dad."

I showered and shaved. I took care of campus emails. I brought Zorro outdoors one more time prior to the vet. Again, the dog had loose stools and looked in discomfort. I collected a stool sample. I cleaned up Zorro and then got him into my car. The COVID protocol at the vet was phoning the office once we reached their parking lot. A staffer would come out, ask a few questions, get consent form signed, and take Zorro. After the examination, the vet would to talk to me. No one was allowed inside. When Zorro and I arrived at the parking lot, I phoned the veterinarian.

I led Zorro from the backseat and walked him to the office sidewalk. In a few minutes the veterinary assistant came to meet us. She knew the Gerhardt dog and petted him. The assistant, whistling "Let It Go" from *Frozen,* went off with Zorro. I waited while walking circles in the clinic parking lot. About twenty minutes later, a red Mini Cooper pulled into the lot and parked two car stalls from my spot. A large black poodle, looking at me, was sitting in the passenger seat. I checked my phone in case Scripps Hospital had called. The woman driving the Mini Cooper began staring at me as keenly as her dog.

My phone rang and it was the veterinarian who said they were finished and that Zorro was only going through a temporary intestinal upset.

"Normally, Zorro's treatment involved avoiding food for 24 hours. Water should be available all the time. As his stools return to normal, reintroduce regular wet food in smaller amounts, perhaps mixing in boiled chicken and rice."

She also told me she was prescribing metronidazole if the diarrhea continued two days straight.

"Zorro knows the routine well." concluded the veterinarian. "We'll come out with a mobile credit card reader. Not to worry about Zorro."

As I waited by the clinic's entrance, the woman with the black poodle left her Mini Cooper, her dog secured in the car, and approached me slowly. I saw her through my car's side mirror. She looked familiar but, with her face mask, I couldn't place her. My back was mostly towards her.

"Jonathan Klein?"

I turned and pulled up my face mask from my neck and chin.

"Yes?"

"It's Theresa. Theresa Rydell. From the dog park. I was a friend of Traci's."

Her tone was assuming and synthetic.

"Hello, Theresa."

"Did you get another dog?"

"No."

"Oh?"

"How is your family?"

"Everyone's fine. Thank you."

"I ran into Ariel the other week. She's gorgeous and so mature looking. I see Traci's face in her features. Must be challenging to be a single parent."

"Not really. We're getting on."

"Good. That's good to hear."

"How are you and your family?"

"The pandemic is awful. When will this hell end?"

It had been years since I had set eyes on her. Theresa had put on weight and her voice had taken on some timbre. Her hair was jet black with bangs and she was reminiscent of Audrey Tautou in Jeunet's comedy Amélie. Her coiffed hair was not flattering and accented her jowls. She wore large gold loop earrings – loops bold enough for magicians to entertain a theatre. Theresa was studying me as we spoke. How long had Theresa been waiting for this occasion? I was kicking myself for pacing the parking lot. Momentarily, the vet assistant came out with Zorro. I signed release papers and inserted my credit card into the Square Terminal reader. The assistant acknowledged Theresa and her poodle before going back into the clinic.

"What a beautiful Retriever," said Theresa.

"Yes."

"What's his name?"

"Zorro."

"He looks like a venerable senior."

"Yes."

"I thought you said you didn't get another dog?"

"Zorro's not mine. My friend's dog. I'm covering for a few days."

"I still have my poodle Roxy. Roxy reads minds. Very smart poodle. She could have a website and make a terrific profit. Give up my day job."

"What a smart idea."

"You know, I think of Traci all the time. So tragic to have suffered through chemo and be so brave. What a wonderful woman. What a loss. How I adored her."

"Yes. Thank you Theresa. Everyone loved Traci."

"You know, she and I had some great experiences wine tasting in Temecula."

"How nice."

"She really knew her wines. So much fun to be with. We loved the serendipity of the dog park, but spending time with Traci without our dogs was even more special."

"I'm running late. Good to see you, Theresa."

"Happy to see you, Jonathan and…Zorro."

I tugged on the leash and I led Zorro to my car. I couldn't leave the parking lot fast enough. Where was Traci now? Observing this farce from afar? Was I expected to ask Theresa questions about their affair? And if so, would it prove that I was a sadist or a masochist? Was it required of me to tell the queen of the dog park that I knew what had transpired? That my teenage son was the bearer of the news? Doing anything like that would debase my family. Was Theresa insinuating that she had a greater intimacy with my wife?

Bring on Max Edelmann. It was time to take a bullet in the head.

There's an infamous Old Hollywood tale of jealousy and farce in the life of Marilyn Monroe. November 1954 Frank Sinatra and Joe DiMaggio broke into the West Hollywood apartment of Florence Kotz to catch Marilyn in bed with a woman. Sinatra and DiMaggio were given the wrong apartment number by a private detective. The "Wrong Door Raid" fiasco had transpired nine days after Monroe's divorce from the baseball star. Sinatra was ostensibly acting on behalf of DiMaggio, a caring friend to a grieving one. DiMaggio hadn't known at the time that Sinatra was also sleeping with her. The story comforted me.

As I was pulling into my driveway, there was a call from Scripps Hospital. One of the doctors was nice enough to convey that Oscar Gerhardt's eye movements were more patterned. The doctor said this was good. There were instances of spastic flexion and withdrawal from mild pain. These were incremental signs of an improving situation. Gerhardt's family already received this update. Gerhardt was fighting to come back.

CHAPTER TWENTY-EIGHT

Gerhardt's wife Jackie called, energized by her husband's health news.

"Jonathan, I arrive in San Diego Saturday afternoon. My father's situation is solved."

"Good."

"Dr. Abrams was very encouraging."

"Yes, I spoke with Abrams today." I said.

"I know you and I will connect at the hospital. Our friends have been so supportive. Phoebe has been super. So you can bring Zorro back Saturday any time after 2pm."

"To your home or to Phoebe's?"

"Phoebe's please. I can't be distracted by Zorro. It's all about Oscar and keeping a vigil at the hospital. When you return Zorro to Phoebe, could you pick up a few good bottles of wine to show my appreciation?"

"I can do that."

"Thank you a hundred times over. You saved Oscar's life. You're a saint. I'll reimburse you. This must be so hard for you. How are your children?"

"They're fine, Jackie."

"Are they still in high school?"

Barry is, yes. Ariel took a gap year before college."

"Gap years are tricky."

"I realize. I am a college teacher."

"Your wear your sarcasm gently."

"Thank you."

"Oscar's sarcasm is classically abrasive, between Voltaire and Simon Cowell"

"That's an odd pairing." I said.

"Who would you pair with Cowell? Someone live or dead? Are you religious, Jonathan?"

"Yes. Aren't you, Jackie?"

"I was."

"You were raised Catholic?"

"Yes. Maybe it was too intense for my childhood."

"So what are you now?" I asked.

"I honestly don't know. I want to believe in God and prayer. Especially now. Maybe God can only focus on physical laws while we suffer the edge of time."

"Very poetic, Jackie."

"It's from Stephen Hawking. We choose partners for life." she confided. "An act of faith."

"Yes."

"It's a strange symmetry we have." she said.

"What is?"

"Well, forgive my morbidity but you lost Traci several years ago and Oscar's at death's door."

"Oscar will pull through, Jackie."

"The other day I was certain that he . . . "

She made a guttural expression.

"And you can both work on building something strong. A renewed marriage."

"Yes. That's a good way to put this. Oscar and I have to build something better like we were entering a second marriage. You should have been a priest, Jonathan. You have priestly qualities."

There was a quiet lapse.

"I meant to say you should have been a rabbi."

"The life of a rabbi is too much struggle and endurance, Jackie. In a good semester, a professor can sneak by with an eight-hour work week."

She laughed.

"Oscar needs more work. Idle time undoes him. He was once a brilliant writer." she said wistfully.

"I just reread his excellent book on Anthony Burgess."

"It's a classic."

"He wrote with a different voice back then."

"Yes. He was once genius." Jackie said.

"He should return to British critical studies, such as Martin Amis, Iris Murdoch, Salmon Rushdie, Doris Lessing."

"You're so right. Once he gets his health back. Are you dating, Jonathan?"

"No."

"You should make an effort before you lose all your hair."

"I'll wait until my kids are in college."

The swerving of our conversation left me cold. If Jackie wanted a heart-to-heart, her style proved off-putting. She was a calculating individual who had to know that her banter was souring.

"Jonathan, I can be honest with you. I knew Oscar scampered about for sexual treats with older students and visiting junior faculty. That's his only vice. Many respected celebrities do this on campus. You know that. Acting out made Oscar virile and alive. It was triggered by Tourette's. He thought he had consent from women. Those of us near to him looked the other way. We failed him. That's on us. If he comes out of this coma, we'll address this even if it takes an electric ankle bracelet."

I said nothing. I was exhausted.

"Jonathan, are you there?"

"Yes."

"Do you agree?"

"Let's pray that he leaves the hospital, Jackie."

Another silence.

"I have to get off this call," she said brusquely, "someone's trying to reach me."

I assumed that Jackie Gerhardt picked up her other caller. I connected my phone to the kitchen counter outlet. My battery was low.

I reminded myself that I should walk Zorro in case he had the runs. If Gerhardt does have his miracle recovery, I was determined to relay Jackie's conversation. How much did he know about Jackie's internal thinking? If he can revive their broken marriage, will something stronger emerge for both of them? At the very least, he and Jackie could acknowledge their disappointments and their co-dependency. That effort would be worth more years together.

While walking Zorro around the neighborhood, I daydreamed about coming to improved terms with Celeste. Why audit the scars we gave each other? Couldn't we be the improved models of the hedonistic middle-aged lovers in Joyce Carol Oates and Cynthia Ozick's fiction? We could buy marijuana legally and walk the beaches of La Jolla. We could rent roller blades and fall on our asses. We could admit in bed, after long marriages to others, that for a brief spell we were in love.

Zorro moved his loose bowels. I had poop bags. Sprinkling small dead leaves on his deposit, I was experiencing impressive dexterity removing it from the sidewalk. I wanted to embrace this charismatic dog in my temporal life. Zorro had nothing to do with Terry Gilliam. and Jean-Pierre Jeunet. Nothing to do with Wes Anderson and his animated *Isle of Dogs*. In this moment I was unchained from my culture's table of contents. I was the old idiot dog walker. I was the truculent stand-in for an American screen adaptation of Robert Musil's *The Man Without Qualities*. I was my own weird maladaptation. The Jewish New Year 5781 seemed to be a test. The Hebrew letters which relate to 5781, spun about spell variations of *Tav Shin Peh Aleph*.

Tashpa holds the root for *ashpah*, a quiver, which is classic symbol of a brave warrior. I was the archer with a broken arrow.

I imagined going to my first Visual Arts Department faculty Zoom meeting, wearing an old campus sweatshirt as the Visual Arts chair introduces me to the faculty. I imagined that I introduce myself to my new colleagues by taking a perverse, comic tangent on the life of Benny Edelmann. I imagined codifying to Vis Arts faculty Benny's philosophy of money, power, and pleasure. I could rephrase and redefine Jewish Fragility as an incompatible strain of America's White Fragility, giving scant proof that anti-Semites vandalized my mother's grave in 2020.

There were missed calls on my phone while charging it. One was from Lieutenant Woodruff. Another was from Celeste. A third from Horowitz. A fourth from Benny. I was overwhelmed.

I put the phone down and went to find Zorro who was on my bed, half asleep. I sat down beside him and ran my fingers through his lustrous fur. His body stretched completely across the bed. Being close to the dog calmed me. Zorro seemed to like me. I could glean that this Golden Retriever was more than an overweight canine in senior years. He was sent by angels. He would assist me and I might help his owner Oscar Gerhardt.

Zorro licked my hand, my forearm, my face. His wide brown eyes were soulful. To my tired vision he was smiling. He acknowledged that I was spending the better part of the day with him. He was cognizant that he had the runs. Not a serious thing. Everyone gets diarrhea. Zorro knew that he didn't live here, but he was signaling that he wanted the world to be right. Lamont liked to joke that some dogs were failed monks who didn't meditate enough. Many Tibetan Buddhist monks believed that a human being could be reincarnated into a dog like a Spaniel who lived fully with the monks. I was in communion with a compassionate twelve-year-old fighting early hip dysplasia who would leave this Saturday.

CHAPTER TWENTY-NINE

I drove to campus for an errand to retrieve a few books, BluRays and DVDs from my office. My car went around the newly constructed tented COVID test site for all students, staff and faculty. The parking lot was empty and had an eerie atmosphere. I felt confident that I wouldn't run into any Literature Department folks as nearly all classes were online. There was a remote chance of happening upon Jason Horowitz.

My phone pinged. It was Yunmei. Her text was disconcerting. She was arrested yesterday in Manhattan for a graffitiing the Chinese Consulate walls. She was freed on bail paid for by her Union Theological friend Walter Garland. I had hoped that she was regulating herself after her truce with the aunt from China. Again, I had wished that she did her graduate work in San Diego. I composed a short text acknowledging her news and repeating cautionary platitudes.

"Focus only on Columbia studies. Forget politics for now. Call me tomorrow. Anytime is okay."

The only souls around the Literature building were maintenance crew in masks and gloves. A cinematographer surveying the site would determine this campus wasteland as having perfect design elements of a dystopian film. Wasn't it an anthropologist who defined anthropology, "to make the strange familiar, and the familiar strange"? The ubiquitous phrase encased these forboding conditions: long lines outside supermarkets and pharmacies, empty parking lots at airports, campuses, sports arenas, convention centers, and concert halls.

On the drive back from campus to home, I called Celeste and got her buoyant recorded voice. She changed the message weekly, alerting callers that she was travelling out of town. I called Fred Woodruff.

"Fred. Jonathan."

"I can't talk long. We got a confirmed report Edelmann missed his O'Hare hub flight to New York. He could still be in Chicago."

"What does that mean?"

"I don't know. He might return to San Diego on a bus or train, under the radar. If he tries to book a flight, we'd know. Maybe he had reason to layover in O'Hare. See family or friends. Or it could mean that he just wants to increase your anxiety for the hell of it."

"Or rent a car and drive the distance?"

"Yeah. I couldn't guarantee that we'd get an alert in time to rental companies in Illinois to prevent a rental. Or he could steal or borrow a car."

"What should I do?"

"I think you're okay for forty-eight hours. I'll have a patrol car drive by your home twice a day plus an unmarked car in the evening. Maybe leave a patrol car parked by your house for a couple of days. I'll put in a call with the FBI. So keep you guard up. This isn't ideal. You know this guy better than I. Talk later."

This was disquieting new. I phoned Benny. Please pick up.

"Hello?"

"Benny, it's Jonathan Klein."

"I know." came his lugubrious voice.

"How are you today?"

"I could be better. I could be worse."

"Are you eating?"

"Yeah, I'm eating. Everything has no taste. How's Cassandra?"

"She's fine."

"You bullshitting me?"

"No, Benny. Are you on the mend?"

"I walk outside the room a couple of times a day. But I can't go into the lobby."

"That's progress."

"This virus was cooked up by China. Some evil fuck cooked this up."

"Maybe, Benny. Nobody knows."

"The government knows. So Jonathan, I'm still waiting for photos of my cat."

"I sent some a few days ago."

"Never got them."

"I'll send them again to your phone after this call."

"Send them to both phones. You know I got two phones."

"I know."

"Every other day, Jonathan. Send them. It doesn't cost a penny to fucking send them."

"Yeah, Benny."

"Cassandra's very photogenic."

'Listen, Benny. What the hell is going on with Max?"

"I talked to him. He flew to see you. That's Maxie for you."

"Well, the cops put him on a return flight to Westchester, but he missed his connecting plane from O'Hare."

"Are you sure?"

"Yeah."

"Maybe he's got a new girlfriend in Chicago?"

"I doubt it. Did you tell him I'm out of the will?"

"No."

"Why not?"

"Because Maxie doesn't run my goddamn life."

"Benny, I live with my teenage son. We don't need bullets through the living room window. I notified the cops."

"I'll break both his legs if he tries any shit."

"Benny, that's not good enough."

"I told him to knock it off."

"I'll deliver Cassandra to him next week."

"No. He'll kill the cat. Maxie can't care for an animal."

"Benny, I'm scared. The police can't guarantee protection."

"If you lived in Jersey, I could get you excellent protection."

"Benny…"

"What?"

"When are you getting released?"

"Next week, if things look good."

"How often do you speak to Max?"

"Twice a day."

"Take care of Max's issue. Please."

"Maxie's had an issue since he was six. He's got a destructive side."

"I'm begging you, Benny."

"Take a breath. I'll call him tonight. I'll wire him money. I'll get him home from O'Hare and haul his ass to my estate lawyer. But Maxie can't get the cat."

"I'm worried he'll drive to California."

"Ain't going to happen. He hates to drive long distance. Forget about it."

"What if someone drives him?"

"Forget about it. He's not driving to California."

"Okay, Benny."

"Okay."

"Get your estate lawyer on this."

Benny coughed into the phone.

"That's right. My estate lawyer. You like baseball, Jonathan?"

"Yeah." I said without thinking.

"Two old Yankee friends who played ball all through school, argued day and night if there was a heaven. Did you hear this one?"

"No."

"So, the fatter guy Morty says to Slim, whoever dies first must make an effort to talk beyond the grave. A year later, Morty has heart surgery and fucking dies in the hospital. A month goes by, Slim awakes from a dream hearing Morty. Morty is talking to him. Slim can't believe it. Morty says to Slim, I've got good news and bad news for you. Slim says, give me the good news first. Morty says, okay, there's baseball here with a seventh inning stretch, hot dogs, double headers. Slim says, so what's the bad news? Morty tells Slim, you're pitching next Thursday."

"That's funny, Benny."

Benny coughed again and hung up.

I phoned Horowitz and left a message on his voicemail. I told him that I needed to consult the committee on privilege and tenure.

I made myself a strong pot of coffee and sat outside on the patio with Zorro. I suddenly recalled a dream. I was a hospital patient with a nasal cannula delivering oxygen to me. This was a private room with black curtains. The hospital staff had no faces. I found baggy street clothes and escaped by hiding under a gurney. On the street I noticed that one of my legs was shorter than the other. I hobbled as fast as possible from the hospital. The wind made my clothing billow like a clown. A police car stopped me and put me in antique handcuffs. I heard the voice of Søren Kierkegaard consoling me.

I didn't want to return Zorro to Gerhardt's neighbor on Saturday. Animals gave me solace. I was entertaining the notion of getting the cat back from Colby. As I was finishing my coffee I recalled that one hundred and fifty years ago, Kierkegaard was decimated in the Copenhagen press by *The Corsair*, a satirical journal, for his public strolls sporting his short, stunted leg. I also remembered my father telling me that Benny had one leg longer than the other, a condition from birth. My father had emphasized that no one ever joked about Benny's short leg.

CHAPTER THIRTY-THREE

Colby called while I was on the patio. I was about to contact him about more photos of Cassandra. He sounded nervous touching initially on his dissertation, but that was camouflage.

"There was a problem yesterday morning but I think it will be okay." said Colby.

"Was the cat sick?"

"No."

"What's the problem?"

"I had an InstaCart delivery in the morning while I was in the shower. Maybe the guy was expecting a tip. My front door was unlocked."

"Are you saying she got out?"

"Well, yes. But I put up signs right away and got a call an hour ago from a neighbor who has Cassandra. Incredibly good luck."

"Colby?"

"My neighbor gets home from work around 5pm and I'll go right over."

"What if it's not Cassandra?"

"I doubt it. I had her photo on the signs."

"Colby, I hope to God this cat is Cassandra."

"Not a problem, it's 100% her."

"Text me as soon as you pick up the cat. I also need cat photos to send to New York."

"Of course. Definitely."

"Anything else, Colby?"

"I need a short time extension on my chapter."

"Two weeks?"

"That would be a great. Thank you." he said as we ended the call and I entered a tailspin. Colby was always responsible. If we had lost the cat, there will be blood. I should have had Cassandra stay with me. This was my mistake, not Colby's. In this madness, my mind rummaged through films having vanished cat plots with happy endings, from *Lost Cat Corona* to *Inside Llewyn Davis*. Betting odds were fifty-fifty that Colby's neighbor had the right cat. Betting odds that Benny's son would be at my door were not any better. The odds of Gerhardt's full recovery were not any worse.

It was the hour to walk Zorro. I found his leash and my earbuds to listen to an audio book that I had abandoned a month ago, Alice Hoffman's *The World That We Knew*. Her novel set in Nazi Germany explored two Jewish girls fleeing persecution. In the author's tapestry of magical realism and trauma, stood a supernatural Golem created by the girls and a spirit animal in the form of a heron. There were stretches of Hoffman's writing that made me think about accepting metaphysics in 2020. This was a throwback to Carlos Castaneda's 1968 faux anthropological *The Teaching of Don Juan: A Yaqui Way of Knowledge* – a phantasmagorical apprenticeship with a Yaqui Indian shaman. These days my life was upended by Cassandra, Zorro and the ridiculous possibilities of spirit animal directives.

Upon returning home with Zorro, I googled "spirit animal". Apparently, "spirit animal" was exceedingly different from "animal spirits", the latter being a key phrase coined by British economist, John Maynard Keynes, to denote how investors make decisions in an era characterized by financial chaos. One of the biggest "spirit animal" hits on Google was Gwyneth Paltrow's commercial *Goop* website. At Paltrow's site one could find a complete "Guide to Spirit Animals". *Goop* explained that Spirit Animals have other names such as animal guides, spirit helpers, spirit allies, power animals, or animal helpers. It seemed to be a sacred tenet that people cannot choose the animal, rather the animal chooses the human in need. I had suspected that Soderbergh's *Contagion* had Paltrow's character Beth die at the beginning of the story as punishment for launching *Goop* three years prior to the film's 2011 premiere.

Celeste phoned and she sensed that I was concealing anxiety. I downplayed the matter of a lost cat. Celeste mentioned Ariel and her curiosity about my daughter's whereabouts. I said that Ariel, no longer a minor, had unusual escapades. Sometimes she was living at home. Sometimes she's with friends. What was different this cycle was the sustained silence. A year ago, I could phone her friends' parents for a reality check.

"I would be thrilled to see Ariel during the visit."

"I don't think that was in the cards." I said.

"Make it happen, Jonathan."

"I'll try."

"Good."

She denounced the Los Angeles air quality. Fires throughout the west had terrified the Pacific Coast states. Celeste joked about getting a Brazilian wax in L.A. with a Groupon. I wished her good luck with all beauty vendors shut down during COVID.

"I miss you."

"I miss you too." I said.

Barry came out to the patio and said there was a tall guy asking for me.

"Who is it?"

"He said his name too fast. I know he's with the university."

"What does he look like?"

"I don't know. He's got a mask on."

"I told you not to answer the door."

"This dude looks safe. Drives a BMW. You said not to answer if a short guy calls."

Barry went to his bedroom. I went to the front door. It was Lamont with a bottle of Moet Grand Vintage.

"Hi kiddo. I was in your neighborhood and decided to surprise you."

"What's with the champagne?"

"Happy Birthday motherfucker."

"My birthday's next month."

"Are you sure?"

He entered the house.

"Five weeks from now."

"Well, Facebook told me it was today."

He kept his mask on. We walked onto the patio through the kitchen. I snared two wine glasses.

"No champagne glasses?"

"No."

"Got Ritz crackers and caviar?"

Lamont had already been drinking and was laughing off kilter.

"I heard about Gerhardt." said Lamont. "Coma. Tragic. No joke."

"He might pull through."

"Yeah?"

"There are incremental signs."

Lamont took the dish towel from the kitchen as we stepped out onto the patio. The popped cork erupted as loud as a gunshot.

"Oscar Gerhardt is indestructible." Lamont proclaimed. "Watch him rise like Jesus."

Lamont poured two glasses. He lifted his glass to clink my glass.

"I heard that he and the grad student had several encounters with leather accessories."

"Drop it."

"You don't think it's half true?" asked Lamont.

"How can anyone know?"

"You start by looking at her Instagram account."

Lamont sensed he had crossed a line and pivoted.

"Okay, friend. In four weeks, we'll have a presidential election that will mark the beginning of the end of America. No matter the voting protocol, fascism is here. Just weeks ago, that jackass Caputo, the senior hack at Health and Human Services tipped off Trump's game plan. Caputo is pure QAnon, saying – 'I don't like being alone in Washington, shadows on the ceiling in my apartment' and spouting cocksucker conspiracy theories. When Donald Trump refuses to stand down at the inauguration, *the shooting will begin.* The drills that you've seen are nothing. *If you carry guns, buy ammunition, ladies and gentlemen*, because it's going to be hard to get.' Jonathan, we are all so fucked."

Barry joined us in the patio.

"Skip, that's my son Barry."

"Hi Barry." said Lamont.

"Dad, there's someone at the door."

"Who?"

"A police detective. He showed me his badge."

"Lieutenant Woodruff?"

"Yeah, that's his name."

Lamont squinted his prying eyes for unnecessary emphasis.

CHAPTER THIRTY-ONE

I told Lamont that I required five minutes with the police officer. Lamont was uncharming and obnoxious, acting like a syndicate consigliere asking what was the trouble. He guessed that the cops were investigating Gerhardt's overdose. I said it was another matter of no importance to him. Lamont frowned. I turned on some jazz with patio speakers as I met Woodruff who was standing in the foyer. We both wore N95s.

"Hi Fred."

"I thought it best to see you in person."

"Thanks."

"We learned a few more things about Edelmann. He spent a night in Chicago at a Holiday Inn and booked a flight at Midway Airport on Southwest to San Diego. He had a different first name upon check-in and a New Jersey driver's license matching the alias. Police in Illinois caught him prior to take-off because Edelmann fell into an altercation with a passenger sitting in another aisle."

"Unbelievable."

"Lucky for us. So he's being held in Illinois. He's quite a character, Jonathan."

"His father promised that he would reel him home to New York."

"A lot of good that did." said Woodruff.

"Clearly. His father's in the hospital."

"Look, this stooge really is keen to find you. He might get a friend or a hired hand to follow up in San Diego. Stay home. Be attentive. Maybe this idiot's father can be more effective in the days ahead."

"I'll press the point with Edelmann senior."

"Do your damn best, Jonathan."

I nodded in agreement.

"Do you keep a gun?"

"No." I replied.

"Just curious."

Woodruff checked his wristwatch.

"Thanks, Fred, for all of this."

"I'll have a squad car drive by once or twice a day."

Woodruff moved briskly and I went out to the front steps to extend my appreciation. Barry met me in the foyer and asked the lowdown on Max Edelmann.

"He's been taken in after a scuffle on a Chicago outbound flight."

"Good to know. Glad you're talking to the police. Does Max have any goon pals?"

"That's what the Lieutenant asked. There'll be a patrol car twice a day by our house."

"At least the dog's getting over his diarrhea." said Barry.

I headed back to Lamont on the patio.

"Bet you thought I finished the champagne?"

Lamont's face mask was off and I saw his version of a Clint Eastwood smile. His entire face squinched. There was a third of a bottle left. Zorro found his way onto the patio.

"Do you have weekend plans?" he asked.

"Actually I do."

"I was going to invite you on my sailboat. The perfect activity in the age of COVID."

"Another weekend."

"You always say that, Jonathan. We're both misanthropes who can't be close to people – except on open water."

"Really?"

"When I'm sailing the bay, nothing fazes me."

As I relaxed from the champagne, I told Lamont the truncated story of how I flew back with Cassandra and the timing of Celeste's visit. He was most intrigued that my good deed to foster a cat led to inclusion in a wealthy octogenarian's will.

"A million dollar inheritance?"

"I doubt it."

I downplayed the beneficiary range since I knew really nothing. I left out the criminal history of Benny's life. Lamont found Cassandra's fate extraordinarily comic and it prompted him to dust off one of his old jokes.

"Ralph and Harry, two brothers, live with their geriatric mother. Harry has a cat. Harry wins a free trip to London. He asks Ralph to watch the cat for the week. Ralph agrees. On the second day in England, Harry calls Ralph asking how's the cat. Ralph says the cat dropped dead after breakfast. Harry's mortified. Days later, Harry phones Ralph, scolding him for no tact. He tells his brother that he should have said the cat was on the roof, and the next day firemen got the cat to the hospital for observation, next day the cat was given oxygen, next day the cat passed away. So Ralph apologizes. Harry then asks how's mom? Ralph tells Harry, she's on the roof."

Lamont finished the bottle and was preparing to leave for supper. I didn't invite him to dine with Barry and me. His impromptu visit was more invasive than supportive. I didn't care to sound out Lamont on the Horowitz proposition to ship me to another department. I could anticipate Lamont's libertine rant about professors' rights and the dethroning of abusive department chairs. He would advocate that I write a scathing, public letter to the Chronicle of Higher Education to embarrass the university.

Good news followed Lamont's departure. I received a text from Colby saying that Cassandra was safely back. He sent photos of the cat. I sent the photos to Benny.

After dinner I drove to Scripps Hospital. I met with Gerhardt's attending physician. Dr. Abrams, in his long-lined stern face and bushy white hair, looked like Samuel Beckett, except for his short height.

"Oscar's making steady progress. In the last twenty-four hours we can communicate with him."

"That's fantastic."

"There's no set timetable. Functional assessments happen daily. These are baby steps but I'm guardedly optimistic that he'll come into consciousness in a week."

"Is there brain damage?"

"As I told his wife and daughter, there might be. Speech and thinking can come slowly. Memory might be impaired."

Dr. Abrams managed a professional smile as he followed a nurse down the corridor.

I walked into Gerhardt's room, having permission for a brief visit. He was an innocent man in this setting. The image was a still life painting. Pastel blue wall, white bedding, tubing and machines, a tan wrinkled curtain framing a window. Light from the lamp spilled starkly over his body. This scene did not represent death destroying life. Oscar Gerhardt, post coma, might never recall how he brought himself to the brink. Silence he spoke.

A woman in tall boots hovered outside his room. She wasn't a family member. The door was partly open. I was eager to leave but I found myself lingering. This provided a solid view of Gerhardt's next visitor, her back towards me. She had voluminous, brown hair with henna highlights. Her soft leather coat was stylishly cut just above her knees. Her jeans appeared new. When she turned toward his door, I got a better look. Her virus mask was dark blue and appeared large for the bottom half of her face. She wore gold wire rimmed glasses. I then recognized her. Brenda Whitaker had come to Scripps Hospital to see Oscar Gerhardt in his coma.

CHAPTER THIRTY-TWO

The roller coaster week twisted into the weekend. I rose later than usual on a warm Saturday. I was to return today Zorro and meet Celeste for a lunch. I expected to run into Gerhardt's wife at Scripps. I planned to avoid all contact with Horowitz. I had complications yesterday reaching Benny as I learned from North Shore Hospital that he had a relapse and was back in ICU. There was no word from his Max Edelmann, thankfully. I assumed he was working through issues of bail a thousand miles from home. As Fred Woodruff promised, squad cars drove by twice each day which had a salutary effect for me, while less salubrious to my neighbors.

Barry and I had breakfast together, which we try most weekends on the principle of sitting together without an electronic device attached to a hand. We were in PJs. I asked him if he wanted to accompany me as I returned Zorro or if he wanted to go bowling, kayaking, golfing. He declined and declined again. I told him that I would be with Celeste from the East Coast later in the day. He grunted something that sounded validating.

I walked Zorro outside one last time. He appeared very happy today. I asked if he was my spirit animal. I read his inimitable body language. My guess if he had replied verbally: "I am if you want me to be, but do you really need a spirit animal?"

I phoned Phoebe saying that we would be over after finishing Zorro's morning business. She was back from her trip to Orange County and ready for him. I gathered up the dog food and other accessories given to me earlier in the week. Getting Zorro in the car was a sad moment. I hoisted his bottom to give a boost. He trusted me. I had cupped his buttocks. He went smoothly into the back seat and sat atop the blanket provided. I played a Chet Baker CD and detected Zorro's energized panting, with the car window down. His chuffing was authentic felicity.

I pulled into Phoebe's driveway. My gaze was fixed on Gerhardt's home while my car door swung open and Zorro jumped out. I had his leash in hand and removed a few bags. I then took a knee and gave him a hug. Phoebe met us on her lawn.

"Did you two get on well?" she said with a fog horn morning voice.

"Quite well, Phoebe."

"I heard that Oscar's making headway."

"Slow but steady. The doctors are communicating with him."

"Thank God." she said reaching for the leash.

"He had a day of the runs and I took him to the vet. All is okay."

Zorro went effortlessly with Phoebe to the fenced yard behind the large white stucco house. Phoebe sidled back to give a salutation.

"This has been a terrible week for all of us. Thank you for being so good to Oscar and his family. I know this will sound idiotic, but dog and god are mirrored words, mirrored names, mirrored secrets. Dogs help us so."

Phoebe smiled and stepped away to her yard. I sat inside my car to clear my mind's debris, hoping to center the day. Rather than return home, I drove along the ocean and then five miles inland towards horse country in Rancho Santa Fe. I saw Arabians in rolling meadows. I decided to drive directly to the Hilton Del Mar to be early for Celeste.

Celeste in her promptness was on the dot. She had booked a room at the Hilton. The terrace restaurant overlooked the Pacific. Celeste wore oversized sunglasses and a wide straw hat, standing at the restaurant entrance. Her surgical mask was slightly off her nose. I wore black khaki trousers and what looked like a golf shirt.

"You're on time, Jonathan." she said in a sweet lilt.

We embraced. It was good to hold her close. Our masks came down and we kissed. She had on a new perfume, different than her usual. It was delightful. Celeste wore less makeup and appeared very natural.

"How was your drive?" I asked.

"Fine. Light traffic. Google maps is great."

"Did you check in?"

"I got lucky. A ton of vacancies. Has an ocean view and I inspected the fitness room. All very well appointed."

"You continue to work out?

"Every day. Totally committed to it."

We were taken to our table outside. The space was nicely laid out with flowers amid topiary design. Something about the afternoon felt like a gifted respite from October's ordeal. Any guard which I had raised in New York toward Celeste was thinning rapidly. I had hoped that she was perceptive to the changes inside me. We were nonchalant and ordered a light lunch, two salads and an assortment of French cheeses. She chose a bottle of Californian pinot noir and laughed at the waiter's hierarchical opinions. We had sparks across the table.

Celeste discovered that I had hardly dated in the years after Traci's death. This surprised her. She had joked that sex had become more important to her than to me over time's bridge.

"How do you measure intimate things like that?" I asked.

"I don't measure, Jonathan."

It was barroom rhetoric for several minutes which made us both snicker.

"Jonathan, when we make love with abandon, life makes sense. No matter how bad things are. You knew that when you were younger, you knew that when we were together, but now you look lost."

"Maybe so."

"When I brought up the abortion, it wasn't meant to torment you."

We were now on our second glass of wine. I thought about the unnamed baby Celeste and I never had. How did I avoid responsibility? How do I mourn?

"We can't roll back the years. We almost had a child. And that would have altered our lives beyond our imagination. The regrets never end, but I forgive myself. I'm going to tell you something very personal. Tanya isn't my biological child. After years of fertility clinics, I opted to use an egg donor. This was a good decision. A wise path. I love her madly. I couldn't have had a better daughter. We love each other so much."

"Tanya is wonderful."

"Other than Tanya's father, only my shrink knows. Tony doesn't know. I was only pregnant once in a natural way."

I finished my glass but the alcohol wasn't helping.

"You look white as ghost, Jonathan."

"I'm processing what you're saying."

"Many friends from high school and college decided not to have children. Do Ariel and Barry help you when you're down?"

"They help on occasion."

"Are you reluctant to date because they're under your roof?"

"I don't know. Probably."

"Have you tried therapy?"

"I don't like therapists, Celeste."

"Some therapists are good."

"I hate good therapists."

If we transformed into pantomime artists, the message she wished to convey might have landed inside me. But unfortunately we were vain primates stuck with verbal language. Celeste tried another approach.

"Jonathan, I still love you."

She finished her second glass. I took her hand.

"Celeste, there's so much going on right now.

"I know."

"It's more extreme than I've described."

"I can help you with Ariel."

"Maybe you can. But there are other problems crashing down."

"Yes, I feel you're in hell right now."

I said nothing and let our eyes take hold. She made me feel anchored. I owed her more respect.

"The year has made everyone modestly insane." she said.

She sipped her wine and then sang Shakira's *Loca*:

"Loca (loca)
No te pongas bruto, (loca)
Que te la bebe
Dance or die (loca)
El está por mi y por ti borró
Y eso que tu tienes to'
Y yo ni un kiki"

She leaned over the café table and kissed me. It was a transporting kiss which gripped me. I lowered my voice. I wanted to cry despite her comic antics.

"There's a Jewish mobster from my father's world, fighting COVID in North Shore Hospital, and his son is out to kill me."

"What the hell are you talking about?"

"The mobster – Benny – put me in his will and I'm taking care of his elderly cat."

"Someone's trying to kill you?"

Our waiter approached asking about the dessert menu.

"We'll share the *crème brûlée*. Two spoons, thank you." she said *sotto voce.*

A moment of quiet. Two forced smiles.

"I'm in love with you." I said. "And I'm running out of luck."

"Did you alert the police?"

"Yes."

"Can you tell me the complete story?"

"Not now. I don't want to dwell on this. The police had tracked Benny's son to Chicago. He was on a federal 'no fly' list." He's now in custody until bail.

"This is fucking serious." she said.

"Ariel and Barry are at risk too. Anyone can get out on bail."

"I'm so sorry, Jonathan."

CHAPTER THIRTY-THREE

I texted Barry and said that there were leftovers in the fridge or he could order a pizza delivery. He knew that I wouldn't be home for dinner. I said that I might be out late but could come back earlier if necessary. He didn't raise any questions. My worry was the remote threat that a proxy for Max Edelmann might show at our door. Barry wasn't alarmed and said that one of his friends would be over to watch a film on Netflix. He offered to sleep at a friend's house for the night too.

Celeste and I walked the beach at Del Mar after lunch. Kelp was everywhere but not many sunbathers. The placid mood was welcoming. She said that she kept an old photo of me in her Joseph Cornell-styled glass box mixed with detritus from our time together. I told her that I always liked Cornell's work.

Along the beach, I spoke about the inimical queen of our dog park. At first, this seemed to amuse Celeste although she was extremely empathic about where the story was heading. Celeste thought Theresa Rydell would be a perfect character study for a Stephen King novel. I said that Theresa's mystique and self-entitlement would be best rendered in a LeAnn Rimes country-style song. Celeste complimented me for knowing LeAnn Rimes but the serious side of presenting Traci's hidden life hit me hard a second time.

We got into my car to see some country estates which catapulted us back decades ago when we drove around the Housatonic River valley in Connecticut. I was losing so much inner tension this afternoon. Celeste reminisced about when she met the late Justice Ruth Bader

Ginsberg in Connecticut at a charity benefit and spoke with her in the auditorium's green room. Celeste professed that was greater than all of her celebrity encounters. I listened to her for the sheer pleasure of her voice. Our conversation was the opposite of interrogation. Still, Celeste had seized on the bread crumbs which led back to Benny.

"My father met him before there were color TVs and ATM machines."

"But you father wasn't on the wrong side of the law?"

"That's my understanding."

"So how do these two men share common ground?"

"It's like the subplot of Bellow's *Humboldt's Gift*."

"Never read it."

"In the novel, there's a gangster, Rinaldo Cantabile, who forces an incongruous friendship with a rising playwright and screenwriter Charlie Citrine. Citrine didn't cross the line. But I don't know to this day what the fuck my father did."

"You're saying your father took a beating for some scumbag?"

"My father never mentioned it, but he had a little gangster personality in his twenties."

"And this Bronx asshole said your Dad knocked the shit out of some truckdriver?"

I pulled the car off the road and parked on the shoulder. We were by an enormous Rancho Santa Fe home that had an equestrian ring and several regal horses. I reached for Celeste to kiss her passionately. I had tears welling up.

"Jonathan, this is so fucked up."

I kissed her again. I told her that Benny's deranged son was in custody in Chicago and said strenuously that the worst was over with the Edelmanns. I brought up all the salient details including the Cassandra thread. We both posited that this election year, a season of quintessential crises, was the inflection point for all the world.

We ordered a light dinner at the hotel restaurant. She kept her promise not to bring up her arrangements ahead to assure her divorce. We polished off an expensive bottle of wine. Our inhibitions were fading. Celeste invited me to her room. I didn't hesitate. There were a few solemn moments before she dimmed the two lamps by the bed. She kicked off her high heels. I unzipped her cotton dress. I thought this would be awkward and painful. Her toned, naked back was beautiful.

We made love. There was a sustained lull afterwards.

"Jonathan."

"Yeah."

"This fucking idiot is in custody in Chicago?"

"Yes."

"Thank God."

"Thank God."

"You are staying the night?"

"Why are you asking?"

"Just answer me."

"Yes." I said.

Celeste got out of bed and went to the door.

"What are you doing?"

"I'm flipping the goddamn sign to keep out housekeeping."

The next morning Celeste showered before I got out of bed. She made coffee. We made love a second time with the sun filling the room. We ordered room service. Eggs benedict. It was a wonderful breakfast. I had a half-conscious impulse to walk the dog. There was no dog. No cat to feed.

"I just read on my phone that Trump, when he left Walter Reed Hospital, wanted to rip off his white dress shirt revealing a Superman shirt. His aids stopped him." Celeste said.

"But he wears red jockeys?"

"Red states, red shorts. What's the day like for you?"

"I should check in with Barry. I need a change of clothes."

"And then?"

"And then we can look for more winding roads?"

Celeste leaned across the bed and kissed my neck.

I showered, got dressed, and drove home. All the palm trees I passed appeared to be waving peacefully in the wind. Long Island had no palm trees, only stately maples. The Pacific landscape branded the other lifestyle, free of intensity. When I got home, Barry was in his bedroom. I heard him laughing hysterically in his online chatter with a gamer buddy. Barry was viewing YouTube gags in the sick spirit of Jeff Tremaine and Johnny Knoxville's *Jackass* franchise.

Having shaved, changed clothes, and talked for a few minutes with Barry, I went to my office to skim through campus email and send my teaching assistants information for next week's classes.

I heard the doorbell as my computer was booting up. When I opened the door, there was a short, chunky guy in a three-piece, ink black business suit. His trim moustache made an impression and he looked like a mortician. He stood several feet from the front steps. He presented a weak smile and a cream-colored, textured business card. There was no face mask around his fat neck.

"Hello, Mr. Klein." he said in a familiar voice.

"Hello." I replied.

I looked at the card. In a brush script font the name, Max Edelmann, filled the off-white space. It listed his MBA degree.

"Do you want to step out or do I come in?"

"I really don't know what to say, Max."

"I know your son is inside."

"Leave my son out of this." I spoke in a low volume, stepping out of the house.

"Sure thing."

We stared at one another like a truly bad blind date. That animal question, fight or flight, ran through my blood.

"Benny thinks you're the other son. That's a fucking knife in my heart."

"Your father has only one son, Max. Don't be an asshole."

"I'm not an asshole."

"I know."

"I'm here for the cat. No one gets hurt."

"Where did you get your MBA?"

"Rutgers."

"Are you carrying a gun?"

"What do you think?"

"I think you got a new gun."

"Yeah, well you're clairvoyant."

"Didn't Benny talk to you?"

"Just bring me the cat, Mr. Klein."

"Dr. Klein."

"I'm not going to ask you a third time."

"The cat's at the vet over the weekend for observation. She had a mini-seizure."

"You're full of shit."

"Look, I'll get Cassandra in an hour. I'll call the vet to change the plan."

"Where's the vet?"

"Twenty minutes from here." I said, planning to drive to Colby's.

"I'll go with you in my car."

"No."

"No?"

"Just get a bite to eat and come right back."

Max gave this a second of thought.

"I'll hurt your son if you don't come back in an hour."

"You hurt my son, I'll kill you with my bare hands."

Max Edelmann grabbed my throat with his right hand and leaned into my face.

"I don't see that happening, Dr. Klein."

Instinctively I pushed him away with my arms extended. He held on to my throat, applying pressure to my Adam's apple. It was impossible to take in air. I threw a punch to his head, hitting directly his flabby left ear. Max Edelmann stumbled back and lost balance on the front steps. He dropped to his hands and knees, a spot of blood hit the pavement tile. He took out a pistol from his suit pocket and pointed the barrel at me.

"You bucket of shit. I had an ear piece."

He held the gun high while searching for his hearing aid. I didn't move an inch. I was stunned by his presence and each excruciating moment with him. I waited for this bastard to find the tiny electronic aid. Max found it soon enough. He took out a container of hand sanitizer and placed the gun on the front door step. He cleaned the hearing aid with the sanitizer and used his necktie to wipe off the excess. I probably could have grabbed the gun. But I stood absolutely still.

"Max, your father can fix this. He told me so over the phone. Trust him."

"Fuck him."

"And fuck you." I said.

"Get your ass to the veterinarian. You got forty-five minutes."

As he said this, Barry came to the front door which was not closed. He looked at Max and me. He could see Max's ear bleeding.

"I called the cops, Dad." said Barry.

"This your son?" Max asked as if we were on a sickening ocean cruise.

"Yeah." said Barry. "You must be that turd Max."

Max inserted his left hearing aid with one hand, grabbed the gun with the other.

"Barry, clear out." I insisted.

"I'm bipolar." Max said. "You cranking me up and that's bad news."

"I'm going to hang with you." Barry said.

"Max, if you leave now, it's as if nothing bad happened. If you don't leave..."

A police car turned the corner, without sirens but red lights on. I saw the car before Max did.

"Talk to Benny. Just talk to Benny." I said in a near stutter.

Two cops swiftly got out of their car and ordered Max to put the gun down. Max halted but didn't drop the gun immediately. The cops had their guns drawn and gave Max one more chance. He let go of the weapon and threw his stubby hands into the air.

CHAPTER THIRTY-FOUR

The police brought Max Edelmann to the precinct for booking. I had given a full statement to the officers before they left our home. Barry corroborated the account. We both knew that things could have flipped in a terrible way. Barry didn't want to talk about the incident with me that morning. He made his way back to his bedroom but left his door ajar. It was life as usual again. I went to the bathroom to check my neck in the mirror. There were a few scratch marks, under my shirt collar. Max's odor, that repugnant mixture of heavy cologne and fetid perspiration, filled my nostrils. I sat inside my office to find something to help my transition. Loose papers, a book, a magazine. Nothing became apparent. I kept reliving the gun skirmish. I was never the target of a pointed firing arm. I did not want to die.

Fred Woodruff called to check on the aftermath of Max Edelmann. He knew of the arrest. Woodruff reiterated that this annoying affair was getting weirder by the hour and I should continue to practice home security. He recommended installing an alarm with video cameras. As it was getting close to five o'clock, I poured myself a tall whiskey. With a few sips there was a sense of comfort.

My phone rang displaying a New York City area code 718. I was curious enough to accept the call. It was Yunmei's theological friend Walter Garland. He spoke with a slight stutter. I assumed there were more criminal activites from Yunmei aimed at the Chinese Consulate.

"Professor Klein. Yunmei gave me your phone number in case of emergencies."

"Yes, Walter. What happened?"

He was breathing with effort.

"Yunmei and I had a few dates. I don't know her that well. I really don't."

"Walter?"

"She and I were going downtown by subway from Columbia yesterday."

He stopped speaking.

"Yes?" I said.

"And as the train came in, a mentally ill man pushed Yunmei onto the tracks."

"Oh my God..."

I dropped my reading glasses under my chair and fell to my knees. Walter said Yunmei died instantly. He said there was massive media coverage assuming this was an anti-Asian assault. Columbia had contacted Yunmei's family. Walter was questioned relentlessly by the police. Many subway witnesses came forward. He gave me the email addresses of Yunmei's parents. His horror infused each word. Walter didn't know what funeral arrangements were in the works and he had great difficulty saying anything more. He believed Yunmei's body was being flown to Shanghai.

Walter described the day he first met Yunmei. He wanted to fall in love with her. He wanted her permission. He loved her. I told him that I understood. I said that I would check back with him in a few days. We ended the conversation without formality. I drank more scotch. Nothing kept the pain away. I read through Yunmei's recent emails and her texts to me over the last few months. One text had the photo of us on Morningside Drive. I watched her films on Vimeo. My hands were shaking. I was in horrible disbelief. I felt responsible for her death.

An hour later I called North Shore Hospital. The hospital told me that Benny was still in ICU. I spilled my last glass of scotch on my trousers and clocked in a migraine.

The doorbell rang. I was slow to cross to the door and I looked out the side window. It occurred to me why people who hate guns still keep firearms in their homes. Parked by the curb was a black Honda Civic. I feared one of Max Edelmann's freelance goons was next to attack and I was numb. It turned out to be Ariel. She was at the front steps, her patterned cloth mask around her neck. I became self-conscious of my alcohol consumption. Ariel looked tanned, healthy and summerlike. She resembled Traci today. Her face was beautiful. Ariel was humming a song. Like Walter's phone call, this did not feel real. I opened the door.

"Hi Dad." she said.

"Hi Ariel."

"Can we talk?"

I nodded. She sauntered in and I followed her to the living room. She stepped closer and wrapped her arms around me.

"How are you?"

"I'm okay." I said.

"You seem upset, Dad."

"I'm not."

"Are you sure? You look like you had an Uber ride from hell."

"It was a crazy morning. A lot of bad stuff. And I just got news that one of my former students died in Manhattan."

"Oh shit. That's terrible."

"It's tragic. Someone pushed her into the path of a subway train. A gifted student from China."

Ariel said nothing. She was floored by what I said and sat on the sofa. Her face turned white.

"Barry home?"

"Yeah."

"Heard you got a cat and a dog."

"No."

"No?"

"I was just helping out. For a few days. There are no animals in the house."

"You should get a dog, Dad."

"Maybe someday."

"You look all shook up. I'm really sorry about your student."

"Thank you."

"I want to talk to you about community college. I think I'll do okay with fashion design."

"Fashion design." I echoed back.

"I could start this spring. I know the whole fucking year is online. Excuse my language."

"Which college are you thinking about?"

"Santa Monica Community College. I want to live in L.A. because I'm sick of San Diego."

"Do you have friends in L.A.?"

"Yes and no."

"Are you thinking of an apartment in L.A.?"

"Yeah. Santa Monica. Is that okay?"

"Why don't you stay in San Diego for now? It's all online instruction this year."

"I don't know, Dad. I'm tired of San Diego and I have a screwed-up relationship with this guy."

"Which guy, Ariel?"

"You know which guy."

"Tommy?"

"Yeah, it's Tommy. He's back. I know you hate his guts."

"I never said that."

"You did."

"Never."

"Let's not fight, Dad. I didn't come here to fight."

"Okay, Ariel."

"Tommy's different after his juvenile detention."

"I'm glad for Tommy."

"No, you're not. I can hear it in your voice."

"Can I ask you one thing, Ariel?"

"What?"

"Why aren't you living under this roof?"

"Why?"

"Yes, why?"

"Because you're so controlling."

"Am I?"

"You've always been like my remote-control device with four triple A batteries."

"Where are you staying?"

"Since the fight I had with Tommy, I'm at Kiana's."

"Who's Kiana?"

"She works at the Brigantine on Shelter Island. Where I work. They have patios. No indoor dining."

"Are you taking precautions with this virus?"

"Yeah, of course. I have a zillion medical masks. Do you need any?"

"No."

"I love you, Dad. I really do. I need to tell you this more often. I know I forgot your birthday last year. I want you to love me as much as I love you."

"I love you, Ariel. You know that. Every day."

"Thanks, Dad."

There was a pause. In the bright morning light, she looked like Traci.

"Dad, one day in the future you'll leave your fog. Really. One day your head won't be spinning. One day you won't be so hard on Barry and me. One day you'll see me getting major design awards and you'll feel so fucking proud. You'll be bragging about me to all your pompous campus friends. You'll stop judging me and figure out why you became a father. One day. One day. I'm much more than you think I am."

"I'm waiting for that day as much as you are."

"Good."

"Good." I echoed.

"I know you're still a mess since Mom died. I tried to be there for you that whole year you fell apart. You know that."

"I know that. Yes."

"I cheered you up."

"I know."

"I cooked for you and Barry."

"I know."

"I did the laundry. Bought the groceries. I sang to you at night. I left you silly notes in the bathroom."

She did all these things. Ariel was a force of nature years ago. She was involved with saving us from our oblivion. The greatest puzzle in our family history centered on Ariel's flight from home at age sixteen.

"I need more money, Dad."

"I'll give you money for college, Ariel. That includes living costs."

"I know."

"Okay."

"College starts in 2021."

"College could start right now."

"What's another few months, Dad?"

"I don't like gap years, Ariel."

"I don't like gap families either, Dad. Fuck COVID."

"I didn't cause COVID."

"So?"

"Ariel, I gave you ten thousand dollars in the last six months."

"I know."

"I can't throw money out the window while you act like a rolling stone."

"What the hell does that mean, Dad?"

Ariel and I suddenly fell still.

"Honey, you're hustling me and I can't do this anymore. I love you with all my heart, but I don't love what you're doing to yourself. Or what you're doing to our family."

"I'm not doing drugs."

"How do I know that's true?"

"Fuck you, Dad."

"Ariel, you must know I love you."

"If you love me, you wouldn't put conditions on top of conditions."

"There aren't many conditions. You can live at home and save money. Or you can go to college and I'll support you."

"I'm not going to do online college bullshit, Dad. I'm an artist. I draw. I paint. I'm a wizard with fabrics at the sewing machine."

"Honey, would it be different today if Mom were alive?"

"What?"

"Would life be different? Would you be different?"

"What does Mom have to do with this?"

"Everything."

"I loved her as much as you loved her." she said pulling close to me, hugging me.

"I know, Ariel."

Everything turned blue.

"You have a ton of money. I'm struggling. There's no steady work. The country's going down the toilet."

"Start college now, honey."

"Okay. I will. This spring. Trust me. Say it."

"I want to trust you."

"Dad, I need a thousand dollars today. If you don't have it, we could drive to a few ATMs."

Barry walked downstairs and was about to go into the kitchen.

"It's not too late to start community college this week. They allow late adds. I can help you with the online admissions application. You know I have connections to several community colleges."

"You don't get it." said Ariel, adjusting her halter top.

"I wish Mom were here. I wish she were alive, Ariel."

"Me too." she spoke softly. "She would give me cash without a lecture."

"How many nights do you work?"

"Three nights."

"That can't pay enough to live alone."

"That's right."

"Is Tommy working?"

"Off and on."

"What does he do?"

"He delivers marijuana."

"For a legit shop?"

"No. Legit shops pay shit."

"How would I know? Why did he go to juvenile detention?"

"Why do you ask this question a thousand times?"

"Because I never get an answer."

"Come on, Dad. This is stupid."

"What is stupid?"

"You're not a detective, so let's move on."

"Why did he go to juvenile detention?"

"You really, really, really, want to know?"

"Yeah, Ariel."

"His fucking parents called the cops after he borrowed their Mercedes."

"You're kidding."

"No. His parents are shit. Two gay guys who adopted him."

"I didn't know."

"Now you know."

"What else can you tell me?"

"What else do you want to hear?"

I wanted to laugh but suppressed the urge.

"Why do you like him?"

"Because he's nothing like you. I got to go. Maybe I'll phone you tomorrow."

Ariel spun around and left the house.

She said things that stung. I should be immune by now, but the reverberations were thundering. I stood cold like a museum statue. My legs could not move. My heart stopped beating. I lost all sensation in my body. I wished that I could restart the conversation with Ariel. If only Ariel could grant an hour of open dialogue without hustling. I would give everything to be with Ariel when she was twelve or thirteen or fourteen. She might change for the better in a few years. My heart was overwhelmed by her presence. Ariel had to have known that.

And I would give everything to restore Yunmei's life. I would even sacrifice my life. I had two daughters.

The doorbell rang. Colby was standing outside with the cat carrier.

"Professor, I tried phoning you an hour ago. There's an emergency."

"Is Cassandra sick?"

"No. The cat's fine."

"What's the emergency?"

"My partner Elgin had a serious car accident and has broken his collar bone. He's in Tulane's doctoral program. I have to fly to New Orleans. I'll be away at least a week."

"Oh hell. I'm so sorry. I hope Elgin recovers quickly. Do you need cash? How can I help?"

"Speak to the area faculty for me. I'll notify them via email today. Classes are remote. I can cover out of state. At best, I'll only miss one TA section during my flight."

Colby's tightened jaw showed his anguish.

"I'll be fine with Cassandra."

Colby nodded.

"I'll be keeping the cat permanently. You don't need any more stress."

I picked up the cat case and heard Cassandra meowing.

"I forgot to bring the cat litter and food."

"No problem, Colby."

He walked back to his car. I watched him as he drove off. I closed the front door and put the cat case on the carpet. I opened it. There was a sound of mercy. Cassandra jumped far and I heard Barry coming down the stairs. The year was 2020.

– THE END –